ROMEO

Wall Street Journal & USA Today Bestselling Author

Winter Travers

Also by Winter Travers

Devil's Knights Series
Loving Lo
Finding Cyn
Gravel's Road
Battling Troy
Gambler's Longshot
Keeping Meg
Fighting Demon
Unraveling Fayth
Forever Lo

Devil's Knights 2nd Gen
Passing the Torch
Riding the Line
Royal Mess
Changing Lanes
Bucking Tradition
Reining It In
Fractured Brotherhood
Ride the Wind
Chase the Sunset
Freedom Ride

Skid Row Kings Series
DownShift
PowerShift
BangShift

Fallen Lords MC Series
Nickel
Pipe

Maniac

Wrecker

Boink

Clash

Freak

Slayer

Brinks

Fallen Lords Christmas

Kings of Vengeance MC

Drop a Gear and Disappear

Lean Into It

Knees in the Breeze

Midnight Wreckage

Thrill Seeker

Livin' on the Edge

Blacktop Freedom

Ride or Die

Powerhouse MA Series

Dropkick My Heart

Love on the Mat

Black Belt in Love

Black Belt Knockout

Nitro Crew Series

Burndown

Holeshot

Redlight

Shutdown

Royal Bastards MC: Sacramento, CA

Playboy

Six-Gun
Monk
Rebel
Barracuda
Jet
Jinx
Mace

VII Knights MC: Golden, CO Chapter
Iced

Iron Fiends MC
My Biker
My Savior

Sweet Love Novellas
Sweet Burn
Five Alarm Donuts

Stand Alone Novellas
Kissing the Bad Boy
Trapped with the Bad Boy
Daddin' Ain't Easy
Silas: A Scrooged Christmas
Wanting More
Mama Didn't Raise No Fool
Tangle My Tinsel
Mr. Motorcycle
Oral Communications
Coasting In
Holly's Biker

Table of Contents

Chapter One

Throttle

"Action."

I dropped my chin to my chest. "What?"

Dice turned to the cameraman. "I need to say action, right?"

The guy peeked from behind the large camera and shook his head. "Uh, no, man. Just act like I'm not here."

Dice threw his hand toward the camera. "I'm supposed to act like it's normal to have a camera pointed at me while I talk to Throttle about the oil change in three?"

The guy nodded. "Yeah. I'm not here."

I snapped my fingers in Dice's face. "Just fucking talk to me, man." I didn't know why the hell this was so hard for Dice. He was the one who was the most excited for this bullshit show, and now he was the one bumbling it up.

Dice shook his head and took a deep breath. "Woosah," he whispered.

I would be the first one to say it: Dice was losing his damn mind.

The guy behind the camera chuckled and took a step back.

"What's going on with the car in bay three?" I asked.

"Well," Dice drawled. "It was supposed to be just an oil change, but I started up her car to pull into the garage, and the damn thing sounded like an orca whale. It's on the lift, but I don't know what the hell I am supposed to do about the orca."

I blinked slowly. "Uh, come again?"

"An orca whale, man. The car is pretty much bellowing." Dice held up his hands. "I don't know what the fuck to do with it."

"Find out why it sounds like an orca whale," I replied.

"I would if the owner hadn't specifically said only an oil change and nothing else."

I tipped my head to the side. "Did they know about the orca whale?"

"Well, I sure as fuck didn't run one over driving it into the garage."

"Jesus Christ," I muttered. I ran my fingers through my hair. "Is the owner still here?"

Dice nodded.

"You go figure out where the orca whale is hiding, and I'll take care of the customer."

"I'm not fixing shit until I know they are going to pay."

I pointed to the car in bay three. "Go fix the fucking car and don't worry about them paying. They're going to pay." Who the hell wanted to drive around with a car that sounded like an orca whale?

I walked into the tiny waiting room for the garage. "Who's driving *Free Willy*," I called.

The four people in the waiting room looked around, but none of them raised their hands.

"Look, one of you is driving around an orca whale, and we're going to fix it." I looked at each person, waiting for any response.

"Dammit," a blonde woman sighed. She stood abruptly and folded her arms over her chest. "Just ignore the whale and change the oil."

"You can't drive your car how it is. We'll change the oil, but there is no way that thing is leaving the shop without fixing everything."

She looked around and furrowed her brow. "I only have enough for an oil change."

I shook my head. "It needs a hell of a lot more than an oil change." I heard shuffling behind me and saw the camera crew shooting. *Jesus Christ.* I didn't think I was ever going to get used to this. "You can set up a payment plan."

"How much is it going to cost?" she asked.

"We won't know until we get in there and see what is going on." Who knew what was making the car sound like an orca whale. "We should be able to tell you what is going on in a couple of hours. Dice is working on the car right now."

"I have to be at work in an hour. I don't have time. Please, just do the oil change." She wrung her hands in front of her and looked around frantically.

"Look, lady," I started.

"Throttle," Yarder called from the office. "Fix her car, and I'll work out a payment plan for her."

"I need to get to work."

"And we'll set you up with a loaner." Yarder glared at me. "Go help Dice."

I threw my hands up in the air. *What the fuck ever*. Yard could deal with her. "I'll let you know what's up with the car," I called to Yarder.

I stalked back into the garage and headed over to Dice.

"Owner have any clue what the hell is wrong with this thing?" Dice asked.

I leaned against the rack that lifted the car and shook my head. "Not a fucking clue. She was insisting on just changing the oil, and that's it."

"Dude," Dice laughed. "She's just gonna drive around in *Free Willy* like it's no big deal?"

I pulled the lever to raise the car into the air. "I'm assuming she doesn't have the money to fix the car."

"So what are we doing?"

"Yarder took over. He said to get the car fixed, and he'd work on a payment plan with her. Pretty sure he did it because the camera was there."

"Oh," Dice hummed.

"We might be able to use this whole TV show thing to our advantage. We get a shit customer in, and we just let Yarder take care of them." Sure, none of us wanted to look stupid on this TV show, but I wasn't going to bend over backward to look and act like someone I wasn't. *Tread: Iron Fiends* was going to get the real me and no one else.

"Yarder has been acting nice the past two days," Dice agreed. "He even brought in donuts for the waiting room."

"See," I replied. "When has he ever done that before?" We were going to have cameras all over, but we were going to have the nicest prez in Texas.

"Never," Dice agreed. He nodded behind me. "He's headed over here with the TV crew."

I glanced over my shoulder. "Jesus," I mumbled. "How long do we have to deal with this?"

Dice clapped me on my shoulder and chuckled. "Eight more weeks, brother. Eight weeks and then we get a break."

Yeah, and after that break, we were going to have another eight weeks if the world liked *Tread: Iron Fiends*.

I knew we needed this show if the club was going to survive, but damn if I wasn't going to hate every second of it.

*

Chapter Two

Dove

"I'm not there."

"What do you mean, you're not there?" I demanded.

"Dove, it's Friday afternoon. I just got off of work."

I pressed the speaker button and tossed my phone on the bed. "Well, we can go together, then."

"Uh, okay," Sloane laughed, "but why are you suddenly wanting to go to the clubhouse? The guys are still kind of irked that they searched all over for you, and then you just reappeared without reason."

"That was their choice," I muttered. "And I did say I was sorry they looked for me. Next time I decide to go visit family, I'll let you know."

"I think next time you decide to go visit family, you need to give your job a little notice so you don't get canned," Sloane advised.

"Valid point," I muttered.

I grabbed my duffle bag and tossed it on my bed. The last time I had used it was when Sloane and I had made the trip to Motorcycles, Mobsters, and Mayhem.

God, that felt like a lifetime ago.

"Besides, I want to spend time with you, but I know your biker takes up all of your time when you're not working, so I'm going to be the third wheel." Sloane didn't need to pick between Aero and me. If I went to the clubhouse with her, we could spend time together, and she could also spend time with Aero. I liked most of the guys in the club and could hang out with them when Aero needed some alone time with Sloane. Sure, they might be a little pissed at me about my disappearing act, but they would get over it. "And because I also just miss you. I don't get to see you at work anymore, so I need to get some Sloane time in." Missing two weeks of work didn't really help anyone to keep their job.

I had been fired and was still looking for work.

Did I need to work? No, but for my mental sanity, work was a must.

Sloane didn't know that, though.

No one in my life knew that besides my family.

"Did you find a new job yet?"

"Uh, well," I muttered. "I'm still looking, but I do have some savings so I should be good for a couple of months before I'm living in a cardboard box in front of your apartment." More like I would be good for a few years, but whatever.

"Why don't I stay in town, and I can help you look for a new job?" Sloane suggested.

"No," I blurted. "I, uh, I've been looking for a job all week, and I've got my resume out to a ton of them. I really just need a break from it all, and I thought, what better break could I have than spending a weekend at the clubhouse?"

"Okay," Sloane drawled. "Aero was going to come pick me up, though. Let me give him a call and tell him you and I will be driving in."

"Perfect," I sang. "Call me back." I ended the call and tossed my phone on the bed.

I hated lying to Sloane, but I had to.

I didn't have any other choice.

My father had made that very clear.

Crystal clear.

"Find out what they are up to."

I cocked my head to the side. "What do you mean? They are a motorcycle club, Dad. They ride motorcycles and run a garage." There really wasn't much to what they did. It was a boys club.

Dad shook his head and took a sip of his whiskey on the rocks. "I didn't raise you to be this naïve, Dove."

He hadn't, but I had spent time with the Iron Fiends. They weren't up to anything. "You really think they are up to something with the filming of a reality show? They're just going to try not to look like fools." And good luck to them on that.

Dad shook his head.

"And why do you care if they are up to anything?" I demanded. "I haven't seen or talked to you for months, and suddenly, you kidnap me because you want to know what the Iron Fiends are up to? You're the attorney general of Texas. Ask them yourself. God knows you have the power to." As far as I was concerned, Dad had all of the power with the state of Texas behind him.

"I didn't kidnap you, Dove, and I can talk to them only when I have cause. I don't have that." He tipped his head to the side. "Yet. If I get the Iron Fiends, I'll be a shoo-in for US attorney general."

I ran my fingers through my hair and sighed. As if I cared about Dad becoming US attorney general. "This is ridiculous. I don't want anything to do with your job, Dad. I thought I made that pretty clear when I moved away and distanced myself from you." Being the perfect daughter while living under a microscope was not my cup of tea. I had lived that life for twenty years, and I had been done with it for the past eight. When my mom died, her funeral was a circus and publicity stunt for my dad. He had become the grieving star attorney who was favored by the governor to become the Texas state attorney general.

"I need your help."

"The Iron Fiends are not up to anything illegal that concerns you, Dad," I pleaded. "They are just a motorcycle club."

He splayed out his hands. "Then, if that is true, you finding out what they are up to shouldn't be a problem."

"Sloane is dating one of the members, Dad, not me. I can't exactly just barge in there and ask them what they're doing while we drink margaritas and braid each other's hair." Sure, I had spent time with the club when we had been at the hotel for the book signing, but that was weeks ago. Plus, it wasn't like the clubhouse was just down the street, and I could just pop in. It was over an hour away.

Dad shook his head. "I need your help, and you are going to help me."

"Or what?" I asked.

"Or everything you have will be gone. That nice apartment, car, and trust fund will all disappear. That shitty job you love so much will be the only income you have."

"You can't do that," I insisted. "At least not my trust fund. That is from Mom."

Dad shrugged. "It may be from your mother, but I am the one who is the trustee. I say who gets what and when."

"Mother left that money for me, Dad," I insisted.

He sat back in his chair. "Find out what the Iron Fiends are up to, and I'll sign the whole thing over to you."

I tipped my head to the side. "You've always told me you can't do that. I only get my set amount every month, and that's it."

He pursed his lips. "Your mother had a clause added that says if I think you are ready for the whole amount, you can have it."

I reared back. "Are you serious?" I demanded. "I'm twenty-eight years old, Dad! How on earth do you think that I am not prepared to take care of my own trust?" For years, he had held the trust over my head. I couldn't do anything with it without his permission. I always thought if my mother knew how big of a dick he was being with the money, she would roll over in her grave and come beat his ass.

"Prove it to me," he offered. "You do this for me, and your trust will be yours to do what you want with."

"All of it?" I asked.

He nodded and took a sip of his drink. "All of it."

The phone ringing knocked me out of my daydream, and I scrambled for the phone. "Yeah?" I called.

"I'll be there in an hour. I need to finish up some laundry and pack. Aero wasn't too happy about not picking me up, but I promised him some alone time when we got there later."

"Girl," I laughed. "How are you still doing laundry? You knew all week that you were heading to the clubhouse. And Aero can have you the second we get there. Maybe I can get Dice, Fade, and Pirate to play poker with me."

"I forgot," she mumbled.

I shook my head. "I think you mean you got caught up in a good book, and suddenly it's Friday afternoon with a finished book and a pile of dirty laundry."

"I plead the fifth," she muttered. "Be ready in an hour. I'm just slowly rolling by, so be ready to tuck and roll into the car."

She ended the call, and I got back to packing.

I wasn't sure how I was going to go about finding out if the Iron Friends were up to no good, but I knew I would need to be adequately dressed. Maybe even a little sexy, too?

I flopped onto the bed and let out a strangled cry.

What on earth was I getting myself into?

My gut told me the Iron Fiends were clean, and I wasn't going to have anything to report back to my dad, but there was a little pit in my stomach, afraid that I was going to blow up not only the Iron Fiends but also the happiness Sloane had found with Aero.

I was either going to save the day or be the villain in everyone's story.

*

Chapter Three

Throttle

"Camera crew leave?"

I nodded and cracked open my beer. "Yup. They said they'll be back in the morning, but that doesn't mean we aren't being recorded." I nodded to the corner. "Say cheese."

Smoke flipped off the camera in the corner and climbed onto a stool next to me. "Eight weeks up yet?" he grunted.

"I thought I was the only one who wasn't down with this show?" I asked.

Smoke shrugged. "I don't really care either way, but if Yarder is going to keep riding my ass about not cussing and spitting, then I might disappear for the next few weeks."

If only that were possible. I had mentioned doing just that to Yarder last week, but he nixed it. When he had signed the contracts with the production company, it had said there would be ten club members. If I vamoosed, the whole club would be fucked. "Just stick to the background, brother. I'm hoping once the newness of having a camera crew floating around the clubhouse and shop wears off, we won't even notice them." At least, that is what I kept telling myself.

"You up for a game of poker tonight?" he asked.

I shrugged. "You know I'm always up to take your money."

The front door to the clubhouse opened, and Sloane walked in with Dove behind her.

"Aero actually let Sloane drive here?" Smoke chuckled.

"What is she doing here?" I grumbled.

"She's Aero's ol' lady, Throttle. It would take an act of god to keep her away from the clubhouse."

I rolled my eyes and shook my head. "Not her." I tipped my chin toward Dove. "Her."

"Her hot best friend?" Smoke brushed off his shoulder and winked. "Not sure, but I can go find out. Maybe she'll want to play poker with us."

"No," I called, but Smoke was already halfway across the clubhouse, headed straight for Dove and Sloane.

I turned on my stool and watched Dove.

Sloane, I liked. Never for a second did I get an off vibe from her.

Dove though? Something had been off about her since the day she just reappeared after disappearing for two weeks.

Her story about visiting family was a bald-faced lie that everyone seemed to fall for except for me.

When I had mentioned to Aero about something being off with Dove, he had told me to chill and let it go. Apparently, everyone thought it was cool for us to search and search for the chick, only for her to show back up with a weak excuse of where she was, and we were supposed to be good with it.

Not me.

"She's in!" Smoke called. He put his arms around her shoulders and pulled her in for a hug. "Get the cards."

"I hope you're ready to get your ass beat," Dove laughed. She tossed her head back, and I couldn't help but notice the delicateness of her neck and the sparkle in her eyes. I couldn't deny that she was easy on the eyes. Something I shouldn't be noticing when I thought something was off about her.

Great.

And now she was here to play cards on a Friday night. Well, I guess this was one way to try to figure out just what she was up to.

Before she disappeared, she had only been to the clubhouse a time or two. Now she was here, and from the looks of the duffle bag over her shoulder, she would be here for the weekend.

Her black hair was piled on top of her head, with soft tendrils framing her face. She was wearing a pair of skin-tight black pants and a colorful baggy sweater over the top. She had tan boots on her feet and a huge smile on her lips.

If I weren't suspicious as fuck about her, I would have said she was the hottest chick I had ever laid my eyes on.

You would have to be blind not to recognize her beauty.

Compass, Stretch, and Dice worked on setting up the poker table while Aero and Sloane headed down the hallway to the bedrooms, with Dove drifting behind them.

"You look pissed." Yarder sat down next to me and nodded to Pirate behind the bar.

"Should I be?" I asked. I turned back to the bar and also nodded to Pirate. He refilled my glass and set a beer in front of Yarder.

"You were doing the right thing with that chick and the orca whale today."

I glanced at Yarder. "You could have fooled me when you stepped in and shooed me back into the garage."

Yarder shrugged. "I don't want us to act differently with the cameras around, but that also doesn't mean that we can't try to be better."

"You don't make any sense," I muttered.

"Her name was Poppy. Barely has two nickels to rub together, let alone enough to replace her whole rear end."

I shrugged and took a drink. "I offered her a payment plan." That had been before we even knew what was wrong with the car.

"And she took one, finally."

"What about the loaner?" I asked. We didn't have loaner cars.

Yarder shifted uncomfortably. "Uh, well, I gave her a ride to work, and I need to pick her up in an hour."

"Shut up!" I bellowed. "Not only are you giving this chick a payment plan, but you're also her chauffeur?" Yeah, that was way more than I would have offered her.

"It's just until we get her car fixed," Yarder grunted. "It doesn't hurt to be nice every now and then."

"I think you are going way above and beyond nice for a chick you don't even know and who is probably going to default on the payment plan you set up for her."

Yarder took a long drink. "Well, I guess I'll deal with that if it happens. For now, she paid for the oil change, and her first payment for the new rear end isn't due until the first."

I was mid-drink and about to blow whiskey out of my nose. "It's the fucking second," I gasped. The longest I had ever seen Yarder give someone to make their first payment was however long it took to fix the car.

This chick just paid forty dollars for an oil change, and Yarder was going to let her drive out of the garage in a few days with a fixed car.

Fucking wild.

"You do this for the cameras?" I asked.

Yarder shrugged. "Sure." He grabbed his beer and slipped off his stool. "I'm gonna hit the head, and then your ass better be at the poker table with me."

I nodded and watched him head to the bathroom. Dove came out of the hallway and looked around the common room for a second. She pursed her lips as if she was analyzing everyone.

Dammit, if she wasn't hot as hell.

"You in, Throttle?" Smoke called.

Dove jumped at his words and rushed over to the poker table.

Pirate set another drink in front of me with a shit-eating smile on his lips. "You gonna let that girl take everyone's money when you know that is your job?"

Did I want to spend my Friday night playing poker with Dove? No fucking way, but I also wasn't going to let her be the one to win every hand.

I grabbed the second drink and made my way to the poker table. I plopped down into a chair and glared at Dove. "You sure you're up for this, doll?"

Dove grabbed the deck of cards and shuffled them between her hands. "I was just about to ask you that same thing, Throttle," she purred. "I've been known to be a kick-ass poker player."

I twirled my finger in the air. "Deal me in."

*

Chapter Four

Dove

I was broke.

Throttle had just taken my last dollar.

"Where is Sloane?" I asked.

Throttle chuckled and leaned back in his chair. "Gonna go ask your friend for a loan?"

I rolled my eyes. "Of course not. I was just wanting to make sure she was okay." And then ask her for twenty bucks.

"Then you should have asked where she was two hours ago when she slipped off with Aero," Throttle drawled. "Since you are so concerned about her."

I turned to Pirate. "Lend me twenty bucks, and I'll pay you back forty."

Pirate tipped his head to the side. "I'm guessing math isn't your strong point, babe."

It was; I just wanted to wipe the floor with the smirk on Throttle's face.

The man was driving me insane. And also taking all of my money.

I couldn't tell you the last time that had happened. Normally, I was the one winning every hand and counting my money all the way home.

Not when I played against the Iron Fiends. Throttle specifically. Yarder had won a few hands when he played, and then even Smoke and Compass had managed to win a few, but Throttle was the one with a tall stack of money in front of him while the rest of us had little to none.

I held my hand out to Pirate, and he slapped a twenty to my palm.

"Take him down, babe," he laughed. He stood and stretched his arms over his head. "I am out."

Fade took his spot, and Throttle dealt the cards.

I took a deep breath and turned over my cards.

Flush. A four, eight, six, seven, and two of diamonds.

Not bad, but definitely not great.

I was going to have to pray whatever else Throttle dealt would save me.

We all bet twenty, and I discarded my two, four, and six cards, hoping for some luck.

Throttle dealt me three, and I held my breath as I placed them in my hand.

I made sure to keep my breathing even and not give anything away by the fact I now had a straight flush.

Luck had totally been on my side.

I now had a seven, eight, nine, ten, and jack of diamonds.

This game was mine. There was not much chance that Throttle would beat me unless he had a horseshoe shoved up his butt.

"I'd bet again, but I know you'd all have to fold," Throttle chuckled. He nodded to Dice to his left. "You first, brother."

"Fuck this shit," Dice muttered. He turned over his cards, and he had a pair of fives.

"I think I did a little better than that," Compass snickered. He laid down three queens.

"Son of a bitch," Smoke grumbled. He tossed down his cards and stood. "I fucking hate this game." The best he had was three nines in his hand.

I was next. I took a deep breath and turned over my cards.

Fade whistled low and tossed down his cards face up. "I can't even come close to competing for that," he muttered. He had three eights.

It was down to Throttle beating me.

Throttle shrugged and frowned at his cards. "Well, I have to say you really are putting up a good fight, doll." He laid down his cards and sat back with a shit-eating grin on his face. "But it wasn't good enough."

I looked down at his cards, and my blood boiled. "How?" I shouted.

The man had a fucking royal flush.

"Maybe you shouldn't try to play with the big boys." He gathered up the last pot and added it to a large pile in front of him. "Better luck next time." He winked and stuck a toothpick in the corner of his mouth.

How on earth did he manage to get that? I should have won that hand. "Cheater!" I blurted.

"And now Dove has fully experienced what it is like to play poker with Throttle," Yarder chuckled. He was seated at the bar with Compass sitting next to him. "He's been kicking our asses for years, babe. We don't know how he does it, but he always wins."

"Not all of the time," Throttle shrugged. "I'm pretty sure you guys won a few hands, too."

I rolled my eyes and stretched my arms over my head. "Yeah, but then you came back and took all of our money," I complained.

Sloane walked into the common room with Aero next to her. "So, did she kick all of your asses?"

"Not likely," Aero mumbled.

Sloane scrunched her nose up at Aero. "I will have you know that Dove used to play semi-professional poker through college."

"A ringer?" Compass called. "That's not fair at all."

"It wouldn't have been fair if she would have won more than two hands," Throttle smirked.

Oh, that man drove me crazy.

How could he be so handsome and sexy and then, when he talks, be such a jerk? It was like he didn't like me, but I didn't know why he wouldn't. Sure, I had disappeared for those two weeks, and the club searched for me, but I didn't ask for that. If I would have known that Sloane would sic the club on me, I would have called her and told her what was going on.

"Tomorrow night, I demand a redo." I needed to get to an ATM and get some more cash. I hadn't been joking when I said I was broke. He had even taken my emergency forty dollars I kept in my phone case.

"Oh," Sloane called. "We could order pizza and have a game night."

"Dear god," Pirate mumbled.

"Or Chinese," she suggested.

"Babe," Aero chuckled. He buried his face in her neck and whispered something in her ear. Her cheeks turned pink, and she gripped his arm.

"We can't do that all night," she hissed at him.

Oh, sweet, sweet, Sloane. Even after all of those romance books she reads, she was still surprised by all of the dirty things Aero wanted to do with her.

"I'm in for doing this again tomorrow night," Yarder called. "It is Stretch's birthday tomorrow, too."

"Your birthday?" Sloane called. She pulled out of Aero's arms and clapped her hands together. "We are totally having a party tomorrow, and Dove will help me plan everything."

I pointed my finger into my chest. "Me?" I squeaked. I was only interested in winning my money back from Throttle; that was it.

Bikers had birthdays? And then even had birthday parties?

Sure, they had to have birthdays since they, at some point, were baby bikers, but what kind of birthday parties did they have?

Black balloons, beer can garland, and burnouts in the common room?

Sounded like a good time, right?

"We can go shopping in the morning, and then we can cook in the afternoon." Sloane clapped her hands together happily. "This is going to be so much fun."

"Whoa, whoa," I called. "What happened to ordering pizza? Why are we suddenly cooking?"

"Oh, come on, Dove. You love to cook. You could make that fruit pizza." Sloane raised her hands in the air. "And the veggie pizza, too!"

"Can I get some meat on that veggie pizza?" Pirate chuckled.

I rolled my eyes and stood. "I think I'm going to head to bed. Why don't we just sleep on what we are going to do tomorrow, yeah?"

"Sure, sure," Sloane smiled. "I'll think about it, and then we can nail down exactly what we are going to make." She turned to Aero. "Do you have a notepad and pen?"

"Night," I called. I scurried down the hallway to the room Aero had shown me earlier. I slipped into my room and closed the door gently. I leaned against the closed door and let out a deep sigh.

I wasn't any closer to figuring out if the Iron Fiends were up to something illegal, and now I was going to be cooking for a biker birthday party. Let's not even talk about Throttle hating me for no reason.

Well, he sort of had a reason, but not.

This was not going to be easy. Not at all.

*

Chapter Five

Throttle

"You're going with Aero and the girls. They're just waiting for Olive and Rocky to get here. I'm assuming Faye is going with, too."

I gently set my coffee cup down on the table instead of chucking it against the wall. "No."

Yarder cocked his head to the side. "Uh, no?"

"Aero can handle taking Sloane and the girls to the store. If you need someone to go with them, have Cue go. His ol' lady is going along and so is her friend." It made no sense for me to go with them. I had shit I could do around the clubhouse and the garage. "I can take care of your charity case's car."

Yarder glared at me. "No, you can go with Aero and Cue to the store. We still don't know who or why the gym exploded, and I don't want anything else to happen. We need to be on alert."

"You seriously think you need three guys to go to the damn grocery store?"

I felt movement to the side, and I knew the camera crew was focusing on Yarder and me.

Fucking great.

"There any negotiating this?" I asked quietly.

Yarder shook his head. "Negative."

I closed my eyes and nodded. "Yes, sir."

"We're here!" Olive walked in with Rocky and Cue right behind her. "Is Faye coming with us?" She looked around expectantly. "Where is she?"

Faye was Olive's best friend and had been staying at the clubhouse since the gym exploded. When she first got here, she had been flitting all about making herself at home, but lately, she had been staying more and more inside her room. Last night, she hadn't even come out when Sloane and Dove arrived.

I glanced at Fade, who was at the bar digging into a bowl of cereal.

That fucker was the reason why Faye was hiding out in her room, though she didn't do anything to keep him from being a fucker. The girl had a crush on him the size of Texas, but she couldn't seem to stop talking about her ex.

A week ago, Fade had finally had enough of Faye talking about her ex, Anthony, and told her to put a sock in it if she couldn't talk about anything other than her ex.

Faye ran to her room, and I had maybe seen her a handful of times since then.

"Might want to check her room, Olive." I hitched my thumb toward the hallway. "Heard music coming out of there this morning."

Olive smiled up at Cue Ball. "Let me go get Faye, and then we can head to the store."

Cue Ball nodded and sat at the table while the camera crew followed Olive.

"How's it being on TV?" Rocky tipped his head back and looked up at me. "Think the chicks will dig it?"

"Rocky," Cue Ball chuckled. "What did I tell you about asking that?"

Rocky sat next to Cue Ball. "Can I stay here while you go shopping? Maybe Yarder or Compass won't mind me hanging out."

"Fine with me," Yarder replied.

"I don't think–," Cue Ball's words died when he realized what Yarder said. "You're cool with Rocky staying here? Without Olive or me?" he clarified.

Yarder shrugged. "As long as he doesn't play hide and seek without me knowing, I'm sure we'll be good."

Rocky folded his arms over his chest and frowned. "I don't know why you guys always have to bring that up."

I ruffled his hair. "Because you scared the living shit out of us, kid, and since you're okay now, you have to deal with us giving you shit about it for the rest of your life."

"Doesn't seem fair," Rocky grumbled.

"You'll get used to it, and eventually, one of us will do something stupid and have to deal with the same as you." Yard nodded toward Fade. "He'll probably be the next one to mess up."

"You talking about me?" Fade called. He lifted his cereal bowl to his lips and drank the last of the milk. He wiped his mouth with the back of his hand and set the bowl down. "I haven't done shit you guys can make fun of me for."

"Give it time," I muttered.

"She's not coming." Olive walked back into the common room and folded her arms over her chest. "So I'm not going."

Sloane and Dove walked into the common room arm in arm. "Are we ready?" Sloane called. She held up a yellow piece of paper over her head and smiled like a deranged hyena. "I've made out a list of everything we'll need for Stretch's birthday."

"Faye's not coming," Olive cried.

"What? Why?" Sloane demanded. "This is going to be fun."

"You're going," Cue Ball ordered. "Just because Faye is being a stick in the mud doesn't mean you have to be, too."

"She's not being a stick in the mud," Olive replied defensively. "She's upset, and I should be there for her."

Dove held up her fist. "Chicks before dicks," she cheered.

"But we want her to go out with us," Sloane pointed out. "Now, if Cue wants her to leave Faye behind for him, then yes, totally chicks before dicks."

"True, true," Dove muttered. "What if we just get this shopping out of the way, and then we can get back here to help cheer up Faye?"

"I'm just going to stay here with her, and maybe by the time you guys get back, she'll be up to coming out of her room," Olive suggested.

"Fine," Yarder called. "Cue stays back with Olive and Faye. Throttle and Aero go with Sloane and Dove to the store."

"Pretty shitty that Yarder doesn't think that you can handle Sloane and Dove on your own, Aero," I muttered.

Aero opened his mouth to protest, but Yarder silenced him.

"I fucking said who I want where, and that is what is going to happen!" Yarder thundered. "I said what I said, that's it."

The camera was pointed directly at Yarder, and you could have heard a pin drop.

I might have poked the bear a little too much.

"Uh, I think that is a great idea," Sloane called. "Dove and I can get all sorts of crazy in the grocery store, so it really is best if we have two strong men to handle us."

"What?" Dove screeched. "Last I checked, I am more than capable of taking care of myself."

Sloane grabbed Dove's arm and tugged her toward the door. "We'll meet you guys at the van," she sang. Sloane dragged Dove out the door.

"Go," Yarder growled.

Aero saluted Yarder, and I followed him out the door.

"He lost his shit," Aero muttered once the door shut.

I lowered my sunglasses over my eyes. "How much you wanna bet Yarder is going to plead with them to delete that footage?"

"I think that is going to be happening more than you think." Aero headed over to the girls who were standing next to the club van. "There are the troublemakers," he smirked.

Dove glared at me. "I think the trouble is right next to you."

Dove didn't like me. That was fine. I wasn't a fan of hers either.

Aero held up the keys. "Let's get out of here before the camera crew follows us."

"Good fucking idea." I snatched the keys from him and got into the driver's seat. Aero and Sloane climbed in the back while Dove got in the passenger seat.

I glanced in the rearview and saw the door to the clubhouse open. "Here they come," I muttered.

"Go, go," Aero called. "I don't know why the hell they would want to come to the fucking grocery store with us."

I cranked up the van and shifted into drive before the camera crew could even step out of the clubhouse.

"Uh, isn't the whole point of the reality show to follow you guys around?" Sloane asked. "Aren't they going to be mad we are trying to lose them?"

I pulled out of the driveway and headed out of town. "I'm not trying to lose them," I muttered.

"Then why did you just turn when the grocery store is the other way?" Aero laughed.

"I thought we could go to the big grocery store on the outskirts of town," I shrugged.

"Yarder is going to be so mad at you guys," Sloane laughed.

My phone rang in my pocket, and I handed it to Dove. "Answer that."

Dove held the phone up and laughed. "I'm assuming Head Dick is Yarder?"

"Yup," I smirked.

Dove connected the call and put it on speakerphone. "Hello?" she called.

"You wanna tell me where the hell you are going?" Yarder growled.

"Store," Sloane called. "We are going to have the best party ever for Stretch."

"I know that," he grunted. "The fucking grocery store is the other way."

"I think… going… in the… You're bre–… Later!" Aero hollered.

Dove ended the call and tossed the phone on the dash.

Sloane burst into a fit of giggles, and even I couldn't resist laughing.

"You think Yarder is going to believe we drove into a tunnel and lost reception?" Dove asked.

"He'll be over it by the time we get home. Just look at my list." There was a rustle of paper, and then Sloane was leaning into the front of the van with the yellow list in her hands. "We not only need to go to the grocery store but also the liquor store and then the party store."

"Black balloons?" Dove asked.

"Yes, but I was also thinking we could get an accent color. Suggestions?" she asked.

"Gray," Aero called.

"White," Dove suggested.

"Green," I added.

Sloane looked at me. "Like a neon green?"

"Forest," I clarified.

"Oh," Dove whispered.

"That's kind of nice," Sloane smiled.

"And also unexpected," Dove whispered.

"Just get fucking gray," I growled. She asked me what I thought would go with black, and I gave my answer. "Or pink. That would really fuck with Yarder. I'm sure he wants us to have this biker party in front of the camera crew but would probably short wire if everything was pink."

"No," Aero called. "Do not do anything that Throttle just said."

Sloane glanced at Dove. "I kind of like black, forest green, and a little pink."

Dove smiled wide and clapped her hands together. "Take us to the party store first, Throttle. We're gonna show that camera crew just what a biker birthday party looks like."

Dear god. This was either going to be a colossal disaster or the most epic party the Iron Fiends have ever had.

I glanced at Dove, who looked like she was the cat who ate the canary.

I was leaning toward colossal disaster.

*

Chapter Six

Dove

"I think we might have gotten too many balloons."

Sloane scoffed. "As if that is even possible."

I turned and splayed my arms out. "I can't see the floor anymore, and Faye is lightheaded."

"Told you we should have gotten the pump," Sloane called. "Poor Faye almost passed out on the last of the neon pink ones. I told her to stop, and I would finish the forest green ones."

Yeah, we totally went with black, neon pink, and forest green for the party colors.

The camera crew was milling around getting random footage, and Yarder had yet to see just what we were up to.

Faye was laid out on the couch with an unopened can of soda pressed to her forehead. "I can finish the pink ones in just a second," she called.

"Uh, I think we have enough," Sloane laughed. "You can help with the charcuterie board when you're feeling up to it."

"Bikers eat that?" Faye asked.

"Uh, cheese, meat, and fruit?" I asked.

"Is that what that is?" Faye asked. "I'm from little ol' Mt. Pleasant, Dove. We're not fancy like you are back in Texarkana."

I rolled my eyes and snatched a piece of cheese off the cutting board. "Sloane and I are far from fancy, Faye. I'm unemployed, and Sloane works in an ice cream factory."

"You still haven't found a job?" Olive asked.

I shook my head and popped the cheese into my mouth. "Negative. I have my resume out to a bunch of different places, and now I'm just waiting to hear from at least one of them."

"What kind of work are you looking for?" Faye asked.

"Anything that will pay me," I laughed. At least, that was what I wanted people to think. I hated lying to Sloane and everyone, but I couldn't tell them the truth about me. Especially not right now when I was close to getting out from under my dad's thumb. I might have to throw the Iron Fiends under the bus to make that happen, but I would cross that bridge when I got there.

"What about the shoe factory?" Olive suggested.

"Uh, where is that?" I asked. As far as I knew, there wasn't a shoe factory anywhere near Texarkana.

Olive pointed to the left. "It's about three miles out of town. They make fancy running shoes."

"From ice cream to running shoes," I mused. "I probably wouldn't have to wear a hairnet for ten hours a day." That was a plus.

"Uh, but you would have an hour's commute every day," Sloane laughed. "There and back."

That was true.

"Not if you moved to Mt. Pleasant," Faye suggested. "My apartment is just sitting empty right now."

"You can't move to Mt. Pleasant," Sloane scoffed. "That would be crazy."

It really wasn't that crazy. I wasn't really tied down to anywhere. "Are they hiring?" I asked.

"They had a big banner up the other day when I drove by." Olive propped her hands on her hips and looked around the clubhouse. "Are you sure this is enough balloons?"

"Screw the balloons," Sloane called. "You are not moving to Mt. Pleasant unless I do."

"What?" I laughed.

"You can't leave me in Texarkana," she ordered. "If you're going to move here, then so am I. You can't leave me behind. You are my person."

"Shouldn't Aero be her person?" Faye whispered. "Or am I reading their relationship all wrong?"

"Chicks before dicks," Sloane called. "I will move for Dove, not Aero."

"Who is moving?" Throttle stood in the entryway to the hallway with a beer in his hand and a shit-eating smile on his face. He held up his finger. "Just hold on one minute before you answer that, though," he laughed. "Aero!" he hollered. "Get your ass out here."

Aero came jogging down the hallway and headed straight for Sloane.

"Now say it," Throttle called. He took a drink of his beer and swept his arm out. "Say it."

"Say what?" Aero asked.

"Sloane is going to move to Mt. Pleasant if Dove moves here to work at the shoe factory," Faye explained. "She will move for Dove, not you, but that's okay because you should just accept any way she moves here just as long as she moves here."

Throttle stuck his finger in the air. "There it is."

"Are you drunk?" Olive asked.

Throttle finished his beer and crushed it in his hand. "Have to be after that disaster of a shopping trip, but not drunk enough that I won't be coherent for when Yarder sees all of this fucking pink."

"Your idea," I called. "The pink and the green were all your idea."

"You're moving?" Aero asked loudly.

"Uh, well," Sloane muttered. "I think we were just talking to talk. It's not like Dove is serious about getting a job at the shoe factory. That's a big step, ya know?" She wrung her hands in front of her and looked around. "But I would."

"You would what?" Aero asked.

"Uh, well…"

"Your girl would move here, but only if I moved here," I explained. "Not saying you wouldn't be a huge perk if she moved here."

"Chicks before dicks," Sloane blurted. "I have to stick by my slogan, and I will move if Dove moves." She slammed her eyes shut and cringed. "I'm sorry."

"You're moving here?" Aero asked me.

I shrugged but nodded. "I mean, no, but yes?" I had just heard about the job at the shoe factory, and being closer to the club might help me speed up figuring out if the Iron Fiends were up to no good or not.

"If you had told me a month ago you would move here if Dove moved here, I would have moved you both in a heartbeat," Aero laughed. "I don't care what or how you get here as long as you get here." He ran his fingers through his hair. "I love to ride my bike, but sometimes it's hell driving to get you when it's been a long week."

Sloane cracked open one eye. "Seriously?" she whispered. "You're not mad about me moving here, but only if Dove moves?"

Aero shrugged. "Whatever gets you here, babe." He pulled her into his arms and swung her around.

Yup, Sloane totally got her real-life fairytale.

I turned my back to give them a little bit of privacy and looked directly at Throttle.

Shopping with him hadn't been horrible.

Sure, he had his little jabs and jokes here and there, but for the most part, he had been bearable. The camera crew had managed to catch up with us when we hit the grocery store, and everyone seemed to sober up and just want to get back to the clubhouse.

It was definitely weird knowing your every move was being recorded.

Like it was right now.

"Like what you see, doll?" Throttle called. He winked, and I couldn't stop my heart from doing a little flip.

Throttle tended to walk the thin line between nice and jerk, with him veering off into jerk territory more than not. But I had to give it to the guy that he was not at all hard to look at.

Tattoos covered both of his arms, hands, and neck, and I assumed more than what I could see was also covered with colorful ink.

Yarder walked in behind him and took in the sea of green, pink, and black.

A slow smile spread across my lips. "Yeah, I do."

Throttle about choked on his own tongue when he thought I was talking about him and sputtered when Yarder slapped him upside the back of his head.

I had been talking about Throttle, but I was going to let him think I had been checking out Yarder. Let him sit and sputter.

"What the hell did you guys all buy?" Yarder hollered.

Sloane halfway pulled out of Aero's arms and waved her arm in the air. "Isn't it great?" she called. "It was all Throttle's idea."

"Wait, what?" Throttle recovered.

"Don't act all modest, Throttle," I laughed. "You deserve all of the credit for this biker birthday party for Stretch. What time did you want the motorcycles to come in for the burnout contest?" I smiled wide and batted my eyes. "We can move the pool table to the side, and we should have plenty of room."

"Are you fucking kidding me?" Yarder roared.

The camera crew panned over to him, and he couldn't hide how pissed off he was. Now I understood why he was so eager for us to go to the store and have the cameras follow us. He wanted a break from them.

"Come take a look at the food," Sloane called. "You won't even care about the balloons once you have some of my charcuterie."

Yarder glared at Throttle but turned toward the kitchen.

"You," Throttle growled. He stalked towards me and stood toe to toe with me. "What the hell is your deal?"

I put my hands on my hips. "I don't know what you are talking about. I was just making sure you got the credit you deserve."

"I didn't want you guys to do fucking pink. I was joking when I said it."

I shrugged. "Well, I guess I don't pick up on sarcasm very well. My bad."

The camera crew moved closer to us even though they should have followed Yarder into the kitchen area.

"This isn't over," Throttle hissed through clenched teeth.

I scrunched up my nose and threw him a wink. "I hope not." I turned on my heel and flounced over to the couch to help Faye and Olive with the rest of the balloons.

Throttle was always around, and the man drove me crazy.

If he wanted to act all macho and jerkish with me, fine.

I was there to get dirt on the Iron Fiends, and that was it.

Throttle may be hot and sexy and have smoldering green eyes, but I did not care. Nope. Not at all.

I glanced over my shoulder at him and was caught off guard by the way his eyes were following me.

His eyes weren't filled with annoyance or hate.

No.

They were filled with lust, and he was looking right at me.

Oh boy.

*

Chapter Seven

Throttle

"I fold."

I took a sip of my drink and watched the poker game.

I couldn't see any cards, but I knew Dove was going to win. Again.

She played like I did.

She knew what she was doing, but she also had luck on her side. As long as I wasn't playing, she was winning.

"Have you ever seen this many balloons in one room before?" Compass sat on the stool next to me and grabbed a beer off the bar. "Honestly, man. Are there even any balloons left in Texas?"

I scoffed and finished my drink. "Probably, just not in Titus County."

Compass nodded. "Fair." He took a drink from his beer and motioned to the poker game. "There's a reason why you're not playing?"

I shrugged. "Don't feel like it. I took everyone's money last night. Might as well hold on to it for a little bit."

"Well," Compass drawled, "looks like Dove is taking over for you."

"Looks to be that way."

The camera crew had stayed well into the night, but they had packed it in a few minutes ago. We still had the cameras around the clubhouse on us, but it was different when the crew was gone. We all just seemed to act more like us.

"You wondering what this TV show is going to look like?" Compass asked.

I glanced over at him. "No fucking clue, brother. To me, we're boring as fuck, so I'm assuming we'll be canceled after one season." The club needed the reality show to work to help get us out of the hole, but these past couple of days did not seem promising.

"That's what I'm thinking too, man. Like how much of America wants to watch us change oil and drink beer, ya know?"

I didn't have a clue. I just hoped whatever footage they got of us, they were able to make it entertaining.

"You think Yarder is acting different?" I asked.

Compass scoffed. "Uh, hell yeah, brother. You really think he would have let this pink and green bullshit slide?" He shook his head and nodded to the half-eaten birthday cake. "Name the last time we celebrated one of our birthdays with more than a pizza and a few beers?"

"Fucking never," I chuckled.

"Right," Compass agreed. "I heard him screaming at the top of his lungs last night away from the cameras. Pretty sure it is killing him inside not to be able to tell us we're all fucking idiots."

"I have missed that," I laughed. "My ego hasn't been knocked down like it normally is."

"Yeah, yeah," Compass sighed.

We watched the next poker game, and Dove won again.

"You hear anything more from your cousin?" I asked.

Compass shook his head. "Nah, man. The Bone Hawks don't have a fucking clue on who is after us."

"You think maybe it was a one-time thing? Like just a person we pissed off, and they went off the rails for a second?"

Compass shrugged. "I mean, at this point, I really think that could be a possibility since we can't find one single person that might know what the hell happened."

"Have the Fallen Lords figured out who blew up one of their cars?"

Compass shook his head. "Nope. Another fucking mystery."

Shit blowing up around you should not be a mystery.

"You think it could be connected to these girls hanging around us?" I asked. "I mean, none of this started until after Sloane hooked up Aero."

Compass cocked his head to the side. "But why would they blow up the gym?"

I nodded to Olive and Cue Ball, who were curled up on the couch together. "Maybe it has something to do with Olive or Faye." Those two were the only ones who were at the gym regularly cleaning it before it blew up. "What about Faye's ex?"

Compass pursed his lips. "I did think about that idiot."

"We ever look into him more?"

Compass nodded towards Fade. "He did right after that shit with Faye happened on the side of the road, but he didn't come up with anything."

"How deep did he dig?" I asked.

"What the hell crawled up your ass?" Compass laughed. "I'm sure Fade checked him out thoroughly."

"Sorry, man, I just feel like this TV show is distracting us from the explosion, and something bad is going to happen." I had a feeling in my gut I wasn't able to shake.

Compass nodded. "You may be right. We can discuss it in church tomorrow."

"With the cameras rolling?" I grumbled.

"No cameras in church. You know that."

Yarder had told us that, but I was a little skeptical since there were cameras everywhere else in the fucking clubhouse. The only places that were off-limits were church, our bedrooms, and the bathroom. But there were cameras at each entrance of those places.

"She keeps looking at you."

"Who?" I asked.

Compass nodded to the poker table. "Dove. She's looked at you at least ten times since we've been talking."

"She's not looking at me," I grunted.

"There, she just did it again," Compass pointed out.

She had looked in our direction, but it was a stretch to say that she was looking at me. "I think we might need to get you some glasses, Compass. She's not looking at me."

"Come on, man. You're telling me you wouldn't like it if she was interested in you? She's not at all hard on the eyes."

I grunted and finished my drink. "Yeah, she's hot, Compass, but I'm pretty sure she doesn't like me. She glares at me all of the time and likes to argue with me."

"Sexual tension, you mean."

I leaned back and squinted at Compass. "You been reading those romance books Sloane is always talking about?"

Compass shrugged. "I might have paged through. She leaves them lying around all over the place."

That she did. I couldn't tell you how many bare-chested dudes I had stumbled upon when trying to find the TV remote. I never read one, though. "Well, you can take that sexual tension you think you see, and throw it out the damn window, man. Dove is not at all interested in me."

"But are you interested in her?" Compass asked.

"I don't even know her, and it's not like I will."

A loud, long horn blared, and everyone froze.

"What the fuck is that?" Yarder growled.

"Is it coming from the garage?" I asked.

Yard threw his hands in the air and stood. He stepped toward the front door but was knocked on his ass when a car crashed through the front corner of the clubhouse.

The force of the crash knocked back the couch Cue Ball and Olive had been lying on and obliterated the TV.

The rest of us were far back enough from the front corner of the clubhouse that no one got hurt.

Cue and Olive scrambled off the couch and stumbled back from the car.

Yarder climbed off the floor and cautiously walked over to the crashed car. Compass and I moved toward the car, and Yarder opened the driver's door.

No one was in the car, but there was a note on the driver's seat.

Yarder read the note and then handed it to Compass.

"Next time, we won't miss," he read out loud.

"What the fuck?" I growled.

Everyone moved at once, demanding to know what the hell was going on and who had done this.

Once again, shit hit the fan, and we had no clue who was doing it.

I glanced at Yarder, who was staring at the car and shaking his head.

Whoever this was may have unknowingly hit us again, but it wasn't going to happen again.

Trouble may have come barreling at us for the second time, but we were going to have the last laugh now.

We were being sent a message, and we got it loud and clear.

Now it was time for our response.

Chapter Eight

Dove

"You are not going home."

Sloane propped her hands on her hips and glared at Aero. "I have a job and life I need to get back to, Aero. You can't keep me here like some prisoner," she argued.

"Did you not see the car that drove through the fucking clubhouse last night?" he yelled at Sloane.

I grabbed a handful of nuts and popped a few into my mouth. Popcorn would have been better, but I wasn't about to break up my entertainment to ask if there was any microwave popcorn.

Sloane was putting on a protest, not wanting to move into the clubhouse, and Aero was going all macho on her that it was going to happen whether she liked it or not.

The thing was, Sloane and I already had this conversation while we brushed our teeth, and agreed that moving into the clubhouse was probably for the best for a little bit.

She hadn't told Aero that because instead of talking to her calmly, Aero had flown off the handle.

Throttle slid onto the stool next to me with a cup of coffee in his hands and turned to watch the show. "What are they going on about?"

"Aero told Sloane she wasn't allowed to go home because of the car and gym blowing up," I explained.

"He's right."

I nodded and popped some more nuts into my mouth. "He is, but the way he went about telling her was way off."

"So she agrees with him, but she's going to disagree with him?"

I nodded. "Yes."

"Why?"

"What do you mean, why? He could have asked her instead of telling her."

Throttle sipped his coffee. "When is she going to tell him that she agrees with him?"

I shrugged. "I really don't know. I'm hoping soon, but she could let this run for a while."

"You're being unreasonable!" Aero hollered.

Sloane folded her arms over her chest and glowered at Aero.

"You staying?" Throttle asked me. "We don't know what the hell happened last night, and until we do, it would be best if you guys stay here."

I peeked over at Throttle. "Yes, I think I'll stay. You might want to go talk to Aero about how you just asked me if I was staying. It might help him with Sloane."

Throttle shrugged and sipped his coffee. "Maybe when I finish this cup. It's pretty entertaining watching him squirm."

I leaned back and rested against the bar. "Do you guys have any clue what is going on?" Sure, a car crashed through the clubhouse last night, and that was really scary, but I still had my task to find out if the Iron Fiends were into anything illegal. It wasn't normal to have a building blown up and then a car crash through another building without thinking maybe there was something else going on.

"We're having church in a couple of hours. Yarder and Compass headed to their rooms to rest for a bit since they were up most of the night patching up the wall," Throttle explained.

"Why do you think these things are happening?"

Throttle tipped his head to the side. "Uh, not sure, doll. You got any idea why? These things seem to happen when you girls are around," he countered.

I quirked my eyebrow at him. "Well, I wouldn't think any of this would be happening since you guys are just a motorcycle club, right?"

"Yes," he drawled. "So then the connection must be you, Sloane, Olive, or Faye."

"Unless you guys have some people you pissed off and are now your enemies," I countered. How could this have anything to do with the girls? I was unemployed, Sloane, for the time being, worked at the ice cream factory, and Olive and Faye, well, I wasn't entirely sure what they were up to, but I had to assume it wasn't anything that would result in explosions and car crashes.

"If we have enemies, we don't know it. We're an MC with a repair shop and a gym, doll. I don't think either of those things would piss anyone off."

He was right, but there had to be more to it. "You guys aren't into other things?"

"Things like what?" he asked.

I shrugged and popped a nut in my mouth. "Just things." Drugs, murder, kidnapping: the things my dad would be interested in knowing. "Illegal things."

"You think if we were into some illegal shit that we would have agreed to do a goddamn TV show?" he laughed.

"Well, no," I muttered, "but none of this makes sense."

He took a sip of his coffee. "Tell me about it, doll. We've all been scratching our heads trying to figure this all out since the gym blew up."

"You guys must have pissed off someone."

"Better get Scooby-Doo and the gang on it, Dove, because none of us can figure out what the hell is going on."

I rolled my eyes and jumped off my stool. "Hey," I called. "She already decided she was going to stay at the clubhouse, Aero. Next time, try talking to her instead of ordering her around." Sloane was going to drag this out forever unless I just ripped off the band-aid that we were staying.

"This whole time, you already decided you were going to stay here?" Aero grumbled.

Sloane shrugged. "I'm not dumb, Aero. I know being with you is safer for me." She pointed at me. "Even Dove knew that, and she never likes to do the right thing."

"Hey," I protested. "I can't help it that I need to figure things out for myself instead of having someone tell me what to do."

"That's also just being stubborn," Throttle chuckled.

I lifted my middle finger at him. "You were doing so good a minute ago. Don't ruin it by letting the jerk out of your mouth." That sounded weird, but it made sense to me. "Or whatever."

Throttle tipped his head to the side. "Uh, okay?"

"We do need to head to Texarkana to get clothes and stuff. We packed for two nights, not weeks," Sloane pointed out.

"We can go while you guys are in church," I suggested.

Throttle closed his eyes and held up his hand. "I'm going to let you think about that and the reason why you need to stay at the clubhouse, doll."

I opened my mouth but instantly closed it.

"You get it?" he chuckled.

I rolled my eyes, but I got it. If Sloane and I needed to stay at the clubhouse to stay safe, we couldn't exactly go gallivanting back-and-forth between home and the clubhouse on our own. "Do you think someone could take us to get some things before church?"

Throttle tapped his nose. "I knew you would get there, doll."

I folded my arms over my chest and let out a huff.

"It's going to have to wait until after church," Aero argued. "If we take off while Yarder is knocked out, he's going to be pissed when he wakes up."

"I'm fucking awake." Yarder stood in the hallway opening and scratched his stomach. "I can't fucking sleep not knowing what the hell is going on.

And where the hell do you think you guys are going?" he demanded.

"The girls need some clothes and shit," Aero explained. "We were thinking we could go before church since you and Compass were passed out."

"I wish I were fucking passed out," Yarder growled. "You girls wait and go after church. Then I might be able to sleep."

"Fine," Sloane called. "I'm going to shower while you guys do your church thing."

"I'm good with that as long as we get there sometime today." See, Sloane and I were totally easy if we were talked to like people, and not just ordered around.

"You want me to go wake up Compass?" Throttle asked.

Yarder shook his head. "He's already in church. Fucker couldn't sleep either. He was on the phone with his cousin the last I saw him."

I tentatively raised my hand. "You guys wouldn't, by chance, have some spectator seats in church, would you?"

Yarder cut me with a glare. "Church is for members only, sweetheart."

Hmph, I wasn't a fan of being called sweetheart. My phone rang, and I pulled it out to see my dad's phone number.

My shoulders dropped, and I let out a deep sigh.

"Looks like you got a phone call you need to take anyway, doll." Throttle glanced at my phone. "Say hi to your dad for us."

Oh lord. Only if Throttle knew how much my dad would like to talk to the Iron Fiends.

Everyone headed down the hallway with Sloane trailing behind. "I'll be in my room. Come find me when you're done with your call."

I nodded and connected the call. I pressed my phone to my ear and took a deep breath. "Hello?"

"You wanna tell me what the hell is going on, Dove? If I had known you were going to be in danger, I never would have sent you into that hellhole."

"Good morning to you, too, Dad." I headed out the front door with a glance over my shoulder to make sure no one was around and sat on a bench to the right of the door.

"What the hell happened last night? You didn't even call to tell me you were at the clubhouse, so I have to hear about it from my secretary?" he demanded.

"I told you I would call when I had something to tell you." I didn't have anything to tell him.

"A car crashing through the building you are in seems to be something!"

Well, it was, but no one knew exactly what it meant. "I'm fine, and so is everyone else."

"Are you going to tell me that these guys aren't into anything illegal now?" Dad demanded. "Buildings blowing up and cars crashing into buildings don't happen to innocent people, Dove."

I had to agree with him, but I didn't think the Iron Fiends had been the ones to start any of this. They were all clueless. "You have to know some things since you are asking me to find dirt on them."

"If I knew anything, I wouldn't need you there."

"But what makes you think that something is going on with them?"

Dad sighed. "There has been talk, Dove. That is all I can tell you."

"Anyone can talk, Dad. I wouldn't think you would be the one to listen to rumors and whatnot."

"I listen to rumors when they come from trustworthy and prominent people, Dove. Just keep digging, and for god's sake, try not to get blown up." He ended the call without another word, and I threw my arms in the air.

That was Dad. He was concerned about me, but he was more concerned about what he needed for his job.

The job always came first.

*

Chapter Nine

Throttle

"Look into the girls."

"What?" Aero called. "They don't have anything to do with this."

"You sure of that?" Yarder asked. "I'm sure you think you can vouch for Sloane, Aero, but in reality, there is no way you know everything about her."

"She has nothing to do with this!" Aero thundered.

Sloane didn't have anything to do with it. We all knew it, but we were at a loss on who it actually had to do with. It was just best to look into everyone.

"Well, then check into her, and then you can move on to one of the other girls." Yarder looked at me. "Figure out Dove."

Dove didn't have anything to do with this either. Neither did Olive.

Faye was the one that I was suspicious of.

"Will do."

"And you can also be the one to keep an eye on her," Yarder added.

Now that I wasn't in to. "Uh, why don't you just have Aero take care of her, too? She's going to be around Sloane most of the time, so does it really make any sense for me to keep an eye on Dove?"

Yarder tapped his fingers on the table and glared at me.

"Bro," Pirate whispered. "There are no cameras in this room, so you better prepare yourself for an ass beating from Yarder."

I held up my hands. "I'm not looking for a fight, Yarder. I just want to do the best for the club."

Yarder tipped his head to the side. "Well, you're in luck then because that is exactly what I am trying to do. Aero takes Sloane. Cue Ball takes Olive. You take Dove. Fade takes Faye."

"No!" Fade shouted. "Do not fucking make me be on watch for Faye. Things are fucking weird between us, and I don't know how to act around her."

"Figure it the fuck out," Yarder growled. "So let me repeat myself for those of you who think they can tell me what they are going to do. Aero on Sloane, Cue on Olive, Throttle on Dove, and Fade on Faye. Did I make myself clear?"

"Crystal," I mumbled.

Yarder turned to Compass. "I know you said your cousin and the Bone Hawks don't know what the fuck is going on, but I want you to talk to them. There has to be talk somewhere about us."

Compass nodded. "I will head up there after church."

"Take Smoke with you."

"Fuck yeah," Smoke cheered. "Thank fuck I didn't get assigned one of the chicks."

"Spend all of my time with Sloane, or go to Oklahoma with Compass?" Aero laughed. He weighed his hands up and down. "I think you got the short end of the stick, brother."

"I'm sure Throttle and I disagree," Fade grumbled.

"Speak for yourself," I muttered. "I at least haven't pissed Dove off to the point where she won't even talk to me."

"Give it time," Smoke muttered.

"What the hell was I supposed to do?" Fade shouted. "The chick claims to like me, but all she fucking talked about was her ex. Talk about some fucked up signals, man. I want an ol' lady, but not one who is going to play fucking mind games with me all of the time."

"Whoa," Dice whispered. "Did this just turn into Dr. Phil?"

"Fucking hell," Yarder muttered. "Pirate takes Faye and Fade just figure your shit out, brother." Yarder ran his fingers through his hair and sighed. "I do feel like Dr. Phil now."

"Thank fuck," Fade sighed.

"Well, that's some bullshit," Pirate grumbled.

"What are you going to do?" I asked.

"Act like the fucking world isn't out to get us while a camera crew follows me around." He swept his finger around the room. "And that is what all of you are going to do, too. We spin this shit of the car hitting the building as a drunk driver and move on from it."

"It's not like all of the cameras in the clubhouse didn't record that there wasn't anyone in the car," I muttered.

"Just let me figure out that end of things. We have it in our contracts that we do have say of what we want aired for all of the world."

Compass clicked his tongue. "I think you're going to have one hell of a fight on your hands because a car crashing into the clubhouse is damn entertaining. Scrubbing that from the show might be a tough sell."

"I will handle it," Yarder growled. "Just fucking do what I told you to do, and keep your eyes open to everything going on around you. Whoever walks into the shop, look at them twice. If anyone walks past the clubhouse or drives by too slow, fucking find out why. I am done being on the receiving end of this shit. The next time whoever this is decides to fuck with us, we are going to be ready."

I thought that was what we had been doing all along, but apparently, we needed to kick it up a few notches.

"The camera crew has off today but will be back tomorrow. Let's all work together to get the corner of the clubhouse fixed," Yarder ordered.

"Throttle and I are headed to Texarkana for Sloane and Dove to pack a bag," Aero pointed out, "but once we are back, we can help with the wall."

Yarder nodded. "Get it done, and get back here. I know a car just crashed into the clubhouse, but this is the safest place for everyone to be."

I had never seen Yarder like this before.

Something was out there, ready to pounce on the Iron Fiends again, and we were all blind to it.

Trouble was headed our way, and we were going to do everything we could to head it off before it got to us.

*

Chapter Ten

Dove

"You done?"

I rolled my eyes and zipped up my suitcase. "You weren't kidding when you said I only had ten minutes."

Throttle leaned against the doorway to my bedroom and folded his arms over his chest. "It's been fifteen."

"I'm sure Sloane and Aero are appreciating the alone time." I grabbed a pair of boots from the closet and shoved them into a tote bag. "I don't need more than tennis shoes and boots, right?"

"Depends on what you plan on doing at the clubhouse. Yarder isn't big into ballroom dancing, but you could probably throw in a pair of heels to be on the safe side." He peeked around me into my closet. "If you could pick one pair."

I stepped in front of my closet and closed the door. "I like shoes." Most of them were from my days of acting like the perfect daughter for my dad. Now they just hung out in my closet collecting dust.

I preferred it this way.

"Let me just grab some things from the bathroom, and we can get out of here." I ducked into the bathroom and grabbed both my shampoo and conditioner from the shower. The little travel-size bottles I had brought on Friday were not going to last me long.

"This is a pretty nice place. Two-bedroom apartment on the ground level." Throttle called. "That ice cream factory must have paid well."

I rolled my eyes for the tenth time since I walked into my apartment. "It paid enough."

"Then why doesn't Sloane live in a place like this?" he asked.

I stared into the mirror and took a deep breath. "Uh, that would be because Sloane would rather spend half of her paycheck on books than live in something bigger than a studio apartment."

Throttle's low chuckle rumbled into the bathroom. "Something tells me that is not a lie."

That damn laugh of his. It was the perfect timber that seemed to reverberate through me and made my lady bits shiver.

"No books for me means I can live in a two-bedroom." I opened my medicine cabinet and tried to think if there was anything else I needed to pack.

"But your closet full of shoes rivals a full bookshelf," he countered.

"You would be right if I actually bought any of them." The words were out of my mouth before I could stop them.

Throttle moved into the bathroom doorway with a frown on his face. "Who the hell bought you shoes?"

"They're old," I blurted. "Uh, my parents bought them for me, and I just can't seem to get rid of any of them." I cradled my shampoo and conditioner in my arms and slammed shut my medicine cabinet. "I've got everything I need. We can head out." I turned on my heel and pasted a smile on my face. "Let's go." I stepped toward Throttle, expecting him to step aside, but he didn't move.

He was close. Very close.

"You do know your story isn't adding up, right?" he asked quietly.

"Uh, what do you mean?" I asked. "I'm not telling stories." Coming to my apartment had been a mistake. If anything, I should have insisted that Throttle just stayed in the van while I got my stuff.

I barely let Sloane in my apartment just to keep her from asking questions, but I just let Throttle waltz right in like he wasn't going to question how I afforded this place on a factory salary.

"Just who are you, Dove?" he asked softly.

I juggled the shampoo and conditioner into one arm and managed to tuck my hair behind my ear. "Uh, I'm Dove. Not much to tell." Jesus Christ. What on earth was happening?

"I need you to be straight with me, Dove. The club is looking closely at everyone around us to try and figure out who is trying to hurt us." He closed the little bit of distance between us, crowding me into the bathroom. "How are you able to afford this apartment and just disappear for two weeks without a word to anyone?"

"Uh, well, it really has to do with my mom," I sputtered.

"Your mom?" he asked.

I nodded quickly. "She died a few years back, and she left me a trust. I get, uh, money from it every month." I threw my hand in the air, and he reared back. "That's how I'm able to afford this place." I plastered a smile on my face and prayed he was going to let this just drop.

"Sloane know about this?"

I shook my head. "Uh, no. I don't really like to talk about it. Who likes to talk about money with their friends, right?"

"I'm not your friend," he growled.

"Okay," I whispered. I don't know why he was so mad at me. It wasn't my fault my mom had left me a trust fund. And why was he so suspicious of me? "You're just Throttle, then. My best friend's boyfriend's friend."

"You're a puzzle to me, Dove," he mused.

I chewed on my bottom lip. "Like I said, I'm just Dove. Not too much to know about me."

"Just Dove with a trust fund big enough to afford her this apartment and not need a job," he muttered. "I still have more questions than answers."

My phone rang from the bedroom. "Uh, I better get that. It might be Sloane wondering where we are." And it would be great to get away from Throttle. The man wasn't my biggest fan, but all I really wanted to know was what his lips tasted like.

"I'm gonna find everything there is to know about you, Dove. Either you're going to tell me, or I'm going to dig until I have all of my questions answered."

I nodded stiffly. "Uh, okay." *See? That should not have been hot, but it totally was.*

He stepped to the side, and I darted out of the bathroom. I tossed the bottles of shampoo and conditioner next to my bag and snatched my phone off the nightstand. "Hello?" I called.

"What are you doing?"

I pulled my phone from my ear and looked at the caller ID. My father.

I couldn't tell you the last time I talked to my dad more than once a day. I was used to it being once every four months. "I, uh, I'm at my apartment," I mumbled. "Why are you calling me?"

"Everything okay?" Throttle called.

I waved my hand at him and mouthed I was good.

"Something isn't right, Dove," Dad called.

"What are you talking about?" I demanded. "Are you okay?" I felt Throttle move closer to me.

"Things have changed, Dove. I can't tell you anything more over the phone."

"You haven't told me anything before this, Dad," I mumbled. "So I'm in the same boat that I've been in."

"You're in danger now."

The hair on the back of my neck stood up. "Danger?"

"Dove," Throttle called.

I held up my hand to stop him and shook my head. I couldn't deal with my dad with Throttle breathing down my neck. "Just give me a second, Throttle."

"You need to get to someplace safe, Dove," Dad called. "Things are happening fast, and I don't know if you are going to be able to outrun them."

My head swam, and I tried to piece together what he just said.

"Who is on the phone?" Throttle demanded. "What the hell is going on, Dove?"

I tried to talk, but I couldn't get a coherent word out. "I, uh,… My…"

Throttle grabbed the phone out of my hand and put the speakerphone on. "Who is this?" he thundered.

"Who the hell is this?" Dad countered. "Put my daughter back on the phone."

"I'm the one asking questions here, and your daughter didn't go anywhere. You're on speaker. What the hell is going on?"

"Dove," Dad called.

I ran my fingers through my hair. "Uh, talk to Throttle, Dad. I don't know what to do with what you are telling me." I thought I dealt well with pressure, but I guess the threat of danger was too much for my brain to comprehend.

"I don't know who I can trust, Dove," Dad confessed. "Everyone I thought I could trust, I no longer can."

"I trust him," I blurted. And I did. I trusted everyone in the Iron Fiends, including Throttle. "Just tell him everything, Dad. Everything. I promise you can trust Throttle."

"Not over the phone," Dad grunted. "When are you going to be back in Mt. Pleasant?" he asked. "I can be at the motorcycle club by six."

"We'll be back by then," Throttle grunted. "Though you're gonna have to give me more about what the hell is going on."

"Dove can tell you the basic details, that way, when I walk through the door, we won't be wasting time. I'll see you at six." He ended the call, and I blinked rapidly.

"Throttle," I whispered.

He held up his finger and silenced me.

He pulled his phone out of his pocket. "You will not speak one fucking word, Dove, until I tell you to. I knew something was up with you, and I was fucking right." He swiped a few times on his phone and shoved it back into his pocket. "You may be hot as fuck, but you are up to some sneaky bullshit, and you are going to tell me everything." He stepped toward me, and I backed into the wall. "Just who are you, Dove, and what the hell does your dad want to tell us?"

I took a deep breath, and my eyes connected with Throttle's. "I'm just Dove, but my dad is Russ Finley, Texas state attorney general."

*

Chapter Eleven

Throttle

"They're all covered?"

Pirate nodded. "All twenty-three of them. No one is going to be able to see anything."

Dove's dad was due to show up any minute, and we had been frantic making sure all of the cameras were covered. This visit was not one we wanted to broadcast.

"I'm sorry," Dove whispered next to me.

Was she?

From everything she had told us, she was here to find out dirt on us and report back to her good ol' dad. That was a hell of a lot to be sorry for.

We were all gathered around the large table in church, waiting for Dove's dad to show up.

She had given us the rundown of what he had asked her to do and kept swearing up and down that she knew she wasn't going to find any dirt on us but had to try so she could get her trust fund.

Hmph, as if any of us cared about her trust fund. The club was more important than any amount of money.

Obviously, not for Dove.

"You don't have to be sorry," Sloane called.

"Tell me again why we need to have these two in here?" Stretch asked.

"I thought church was for members only?" Smoke drawled. "Last I check, you two were not members of the Iron Fiends."

"I'm sleeping with one," Sloane pointed out. "That has to count for something, right?"

"Now, do you see why I wasn't excited for you guys to get ol' ladies?" Yarder muttered. "If you two wouldn't have hooked up, then we wouldn't have the state attorney general's daughter sitting at our table."

Sloane leaned forward and laid her hand on the table. "Is that why you have that bombass apartment? I always wondered how you were able to live there, but I just figured you were really good with money."

"My mom left me a chunk of money when she died," Dove explained. "My dad has nothing to do with my money. Well, other than he is the trustee of the trust, but I was working on that. I wasn't lying when I told you I had a trust."

"How honorable of you," I smirked. "But you were going to get your hands on your trust by being a rat." She was going to get her hands on her money by ratting out the club.

"I wasn't a rat because I knew you guys weren't up to anything bad. I just had to bide my time to make my dad think that I was really trying to get dirt on you, and then he would sign my trust over to me," Dove explained.

"What would you have done if you found out we were dirty?" Yarder asked.

"Not tell my dad, that's for sure," she muttered. "And I wasn't worried about that *because I knew you guys were clean*," she stressed.

"I don't think she is a rat," Sloane butted in. "I've known Dove for years, and I know she would never tattletale on people." She pointed at Dove. "Do you remember the time when Gus from packaging snuck into the mixing room and messed with the measurements for the special edition funfetti? We both knew he was the one who messed up all of those batches, but we didn't tell Grover. We took the blame, and Gus got off scot-free."

"Do you hear yourself when you talk?" Fade chuckled. "Or do you just say whatever?"

Sloane flipped him off. "I know exactly what I just said. Dove is not a snitch, and I would know because I have worked with her for years."

"But why did he want dirt on us?" Dice asked. "We're a motorcycle club from Mt. Pleasant, not the likes of a huge club or anything."

"We're the most well-known club in Texas, and we're about to be on a reality show. Frying us in front of cameras could have been career-changing for your dear old dad." Yarder rapped his knuckles on the table. "Shot him right up to the US attorney general."

Dove shifted uncomfortably in her chair.

"Why were you gone for two weeks?" Compass asked. "It take you that long to figure out a plan to catch us in the act?"

Dove rolled her eyes. "It took me that long to let my father actually talk to me. Being kidnapped by my father's goons is a surefire way to piss me off and zip it even when he really wants to talk to me."

"She's not lying." Everyone's gaze shifted to the door where Russ Finley stood. "She didn't want to do any of this. I had to bribe her."

Dove bugged her eyes out and nodded her head sharply. "See," she hissed through clenched teeth.

"May I come in?" Russ asked.

Yarder stood and motioned to the open chair between him and Compass. "Have a seat, Mr. Finley."

Russ waved his hand at Yarder. "Just call me Russ. We're on terms I didn't see coming, but that doesn't mean we need to be so formal. And I prefer to stand. It was a long ride in from Dallas." He moved to the front of the table by Yarder and shook his hand.

Russ turned and looked around the table.

Having the Texas attorney general in church was something I never saw coming.

This dude was fancy suit, caviar, and jet planes, while the club was leather cuts, cold beer, and motorcycles. Talk about different worlds meeting.

"I would like to start off by saying thank you for keeping Dove safe and also sorry for making her betray your trust." Russ nodded to Dove. "I lost count of the amount of times Dove told me you guys were clean." He tipped his head to the side. "I didn't believe her because I got some intel that claimed differently."

"So instead of believing your daughter, you believed whatever this intel was," I chimed in.

Yarder held up his hand toward. "Let him talk before we talk."

I held up my hands. "Fine, fine," I muttered. I could hold my tongue for a few minutes.

"My intel came from a very reliable source. One that had never steered me wrong before, but now it seems that has changed. Not only is the club in danger, but so are Dove and I." Russ paced back and forth with his hands in his pockets. "You know the world is going downhill when I feel safer in a motorcycle club than I do in my own office in Dallas," he mused.

"What is going on, Father?" Dove demanded. "The last we talked, you were adamant the Iron Fiends were who you were going after, and you were headed for the US attorney general."

Russ ran his fingers through his perfectly coifed hair. "My reliable source came to me from Boone Drake, who is the current US attorney general."

He talked like that name should mean anything to us. We didn't fuck around in things that would bring the United States attorney general into our orbit.

"He's been rallying me to take his place. He's getting older and wants to retire on the lake with his family. He, of course, had the president's ear and said he had been talking me up to him. Hell, I was at the damn White House last month for dinner. Everything was going exactly as it should. Boone said I just needed one good case to put me right in his seat."

Sounded like a typical politician. Sit in a cushy office for years and then retire with a hefty nest egg on a ritzy lake.

"That one good case was to take down the Iron Fiends, huh?" Compass smirked.

Russ looked at Dove. "It was like my dream landed right in my lap, and all I had to do was grab it. Boone told me the case would be a slam dunk."

"What did you do?" Dove whispered.

"Boone changed his mind. More like his mind was changed for him, and I was suddenly out." Russ resumed pacing. "The party decided they wanted to endorse Craig Gibbs instead. He's a hotshot lawyer from Houston who's been putting away big members of the Kilmore gang."

"Damn," Pirate muttered. "You can't get me to watch the news, but even I've heard about the gang going down."

"That's because it is a pretty big deal. No one has been able to successfully prosecute them until Gibbs. He's put away three of the top players of the gang in the past month," Russ explained. "Impressive."

"So why can't they just switch over to him and leave you alone?" Dove asked.

"Because he knows too much," Yarder drawled.

"Yes," Russ confirmed.

"You called me this morning and seemed surprised about the car crashing into the clubhouse, though," Dove pointed out.

"Because I was," Russ sighed. "I didn't know I was out until this afternoon. I figured Boone would have his people plant drugs or something in the clubhouse. When I sent you here, I was hopeful you would find them, and that would be it. From what I can gather now, there are things happening as we speak that will tear the club down. They want you to make choices that will put you right in the crosshairs of the law."

Who the fuck was them?

"Then stop those things, Dad. Stop whatever you started," Dove demanded. "You have to. You're the Texas state attorney general," Dove whaled.

Russ shook his head. "This is completely out of my hands now. I'll be lucky if I finish my term without being six feet under. I've got four months before the next election, and someone else takes over as state attorney general."

"Then what happens to you?" Pirate asked.

"If I'm alive, I get the hell out of politics and retire in the mountains somewhere while looking over my shoulder until I die."

How lovely.

What the fuck did Russ Finely get into?

"Was the car crashing into the clubhouse last night the beginning?" Yarder asked.

"It has to be," Russ sighed.

"No, the gym blowing up had to be the start," Pirate pointed out.

Russ shook his head. "That happened before Boone came to me. That has nothing to do with me."

"Great," Stretch drawled. "The two aren't connected, which means we've got two targets on our backs now."

"If I were you guys, I would be more worried about the one I put there." Russ' phone rang, and he pulled it out of his pocket.

"Someone important calling?" Yarder asked.

Russ shoved his phone back in his pocket. "Unknown number."

"You get many phone calls from unknown numbers?" I asked.

Russ glanced at me. "Only in the past four hours. They're trying to figure out where I am."

"So what do we do now?" I asked. "It's not like we can go to the police with all of this."

Russ shook his head. "Gibbs would be all over this to shut it down before anyone got word on it. The guy is that good."

"Just makes you all warm and fuzzy inside knowing these are the type of people helping to run our state and country," Cue Ball mused.

"Do you have any idea what Boone and Gibbs are up to now?" Yarder asked.

Russ shook his head. "I have been removed from all access to Boone, and my secretary called me on the way over to tell me that a load of cases was dumped on my desk that I need to make my priority."

"Why?" Dove asked.

"Bury me under paperwork so I can't speak to anyone." Russ looked at Yarder. "But they are still going to come after you guys. Gibbs putting away the Kilmore gang is good; taking down the Iron Fiends will be the cherry on top."

"We're fucking nobody!" Compass hollered. "We do charity runs for kids, run a garage, and are on some dumb reality TV show."

"That last one is the reason why you're the target. In a few months' time, your faces will be all over the TV, and then quickly, you'll be on the news as either drug dealers, traffickers, or some other evil thing the public hates. Gibbs takes you down, and he's a hero in the eye of the public. Give that man US attorney general seat," Russ mocked.

"Which is exactly what you were going to do, but the only reason why you're pissed off now is because it's Gibbs getting the glory, not you," Dice pointed out.

Russ threw his hands in the air. "Yeah, so? I would have gotten you a couple of years in prison, and then you would have been out. Gibbs, on the other hand, will do whatever it takes to make sure you all rot in prison for the rest of your lives."

"This guy Gibbs sounds charming," Smoke chuckled.

"None of that is going to happen," Yarder called. He pounded his fist on the table. "I don't know what the fuck you are going to do, Russ, but the club is going to be fine. We lock shit down like Fort Knox and trust no one."

"Pretty much what we are doing right now," Fade shrugged.

Yarder shook his head. "Even tighter. No one new comes into the clubhouse."

"Uh, I hate to be the bearer of bad news, but we are in the middle of filming a reality show that is pretty much paying our bills right now. How are we going to be on lockdown while a camera crew comes and goes every day?" I asked.

"Fuck," Yarder grunted and sat back in his seat. "This is the worst fucking timing for the show right now."

"Can't we talk to the producers and tell them what is going on?" Fade asked.

Compass and Yarder both shook their heads. "We are under contract to provide a certain amount of hours of footage. If we don't, the advance we got needs to be paid back with penalties on top."

"So we'd be fucked even more than we already are," I sighed. Fucking great.

"What if you give the show some excitement?" Sloane suggested.

"What are you talking about?" Aero asked.

"Well, we've all watched reality TV, right?" Sloane looked around expectantly.

There was a mumble of grunts and a chorus of nos.

"Well," Sloane drawled. "I guess Dove and I have watched reality TV, and there always is sort of a main story with little ones weaved in. We make a big story that the camera crew has to follow, and the rest of the club stays back to be on lockdown and figure out what is going on."

"Stupid," Stretch called. "We don't have anything going on other than fixing cars."

Sloane rolled her eyes.

"No, Sloane is right," Dove chirped. "You guys obviously can't have a camera crew in and out every day. Sloane and I can go off on a girls' trip with the camera crew following."

"Did we forget about the other twenty-three cameras in the clubhouse?" I asked. "You're taking away one camera and leaving twenty-three. And you and Sloane are not going to go traipsing off by yourselves." Did she really think that she and Sloane were just going to go off by themselves with a shitstorm brewing around us?

"No, they're taking away one camera, the three people that are always attached to it, and two of you.

Those three people that we have no clue about and could do god knows what to us if Boone and Gibbs were able to get to them." Yarder steepled his hands in front of him. "This could work."

Pirate raised his hand. "Am I the only one who is confused right now?"

Dice slapped him upside the head. "Keep up, brother, or I'll explain it later."

"Why two of us?" Smoke asked. "I'm sure Aero can handle Dove and Sloane."

"One-on-one coverage," Yarder grunted. "Aero and Throttle."

I flattened my lips and held back protesting. I didn't want to be off distracting the camera crew. I wanted to be here solving the huge fucking problem we had.

"I don't know if this is going to work," Compass doubted. "What's to say they won't send another camera crew out here to stay at the clubhouse?"

"They won't. I was talking to Garett the other day, and he said they only have four camera crews, and since there are four clubs, they are relying heavily on the footage they are getting from the cameras staged around the clubhouse since there is one camera crew for each club."

"Who the fuck is Garret?" Yarder spat at Dice.

"The guy with the camera on his shoulder all of the time," Dice explained. "You telling me you guys don't know these guys' names? It's Garett with the camera, Max with the boom and shit, and then Adalee is the one with the clipboard."

"We should know these people," Compass chuckled, "but I think we've all been preoccupied with the show and cars crashing into the clubhouse."

"But what is going to be so amazing that the crew is going to leave the clubhouse?" Stretch questioned.

"Well, what normally happens on reality shows?" I asked. I had caught a few minutes here and there of shows like ours, but they never really held my attention.

We all looked at Sloane and Dove.

"You used to watch those sisters all the time, Dove," Russ called. "The Candash."

Sloane tipped her head to the side. "Uh, who?"

"The Kardashians," Dove clarified. "And I haven't watched their show in a while. Khloe used to be my favorite, but now even she seems out of touch with reality. Just not my vibe anymore."

"Still fucking confused," Pirate called.

"Jesus Christ," Yarder muttered. "Just tell us what the hell needs to happen for the camera crew to follow you two."

Sloane and Dove exchanged looks. "Uh, well," Dove started.

"No," Sloane called. "Don't even say it."

"But you know that camera crew will be hot on our tails if you do it," Dove muttered.

"Do what?" Aero demanded. "You two are just sitting here, and I feel like you're up to something."

"It was one of the highest-ranked episodes when Khloe married Lamar," Dove reasoned.

"Am I the only one who feels like we should have watched some reality shows before filming started?" Dice laughed.

Sloane shook her head. "Don't say it."

"Say it," Russ called. "It can't be worse than whatever Gibbs has headed this way." His words were like a bucket of cold water dumped on us.

For a minute, I had forgotten that Russ was still here. He was standing at the head of the table with his suit jacket unbuttoned and his hands on his hips.

We all waited, wondering just what the hell Dove was talking about.

"No," Sloane whispered.

Dove closed her eyes and scrunched up her face.

"Say it!" Yarder hollered.

*

Chapter Twelve

Dove

It was crazy.

Sloane was going to kill me.

There could possibly be other things that could distract the camera crew, but my idea was a surefire way to make it happen.

One hundred percent it would work.

It could also work with Olive. If Sloane was really against it, then we could spring it on Olive, but I really hoped Sloane was good with it. Well, Aero, too.

"Doll," Throttle drawled next to me. "Spit it out."

I cracked open one eye and glared at him. Well, as best as I could with one eye closed.

He leaned close and put his arm around the back of my chair. "Dove." Just my name, that was all he said, but the word rocked through me.

My god. The low timber of his voice and his face so close to mine made my stomach do a swoony flip. Now was the time the man decided to get close when my father was in the room, and we were surrounded by his friends.

I was going to have to deal with these butterfly feelings later. Much later.

I opened both eyes, and our eyes connected. "It's huge," I whispered.

"I think this calls for something huge, doll."

I licked my lips and nodded. "Yeah, you're right."

He leaned back but kept his arm around the back of my chair.

"Uh, well," I started. I cleared my throat and just got it out there. "Marry. Someone needs to get married. In our case, to get the camera crew away from the clubhouse, elopement. Runaway to Vegas or something. It won't matter what you guys do here because they're only going to care about whoever is getting married."

"Not it," Cue Ball called. "I love the fuck out of Olive, but I know she won't be happy running away to get married."

Everyone turned to Sloane and Aero.

Sloane's eyes were slammed shut, and she looked like she was going to puke. *Sorry, best friend.*

Aero tapped his fingers on the table and shook his head. "Well, I was trying to figure out a good time, so I guess now is as good a time as any." He reached into his pocket and pulled out a small pink envelope. "Money is pretty fucking tight, so this was the best I could get." He opened the small envelope and pulled out a gold band.

Sloane had one eye open and tipped her head slightly, watching Aero's hands. "That's a ring," she whispered.

"It should be a hell of a lot better ring, but if I wait till I'm rolling in money, we'll be dead and in the ground." He pushed his chair back and dropped down on one knee next to Sloane.

"Oh god," Sloane whispered. "You don't have to do this. Please don't do this because of the camera crew," she pleaded.

That was exactly what I didn't want to happen. I knew that Aero and Sloane were over the moon in love, but I didn't want to pressure either of them into doing something they weren't ready for.

Though it looked like Aero had been thinking about this for a bit since he already had a ring.

Aero shook his head. "Babe, I couldn't care less about the fucking camera crew. I've been waiting for the right moment to ask you to be mine, and here it is." He held the ring out to her. "Sloane Kristen McDare, will you marry me?"

Oh my god! Could that have been more perfect?

"Aero," Sloane whispered. "If I say yes, then there is no going back. You're gonna have to marry me."

"Kind of the point of me asking you, babe," he chuckled.

Sloane catapulted herself out of her chair and slammed into Aero. He managed to wrap one arm around her, and they fell back.

"Yes!" Sloane shouted from the floor. "Yes, a million times over."

I sighed heavily and sank back into my chair. "Thank god," I whispered.

"Marriage?" Throttle asked. "That was what you were afraid to say?"

I brushed my hair out of my face. "Uh, yeah. It's a great idea, but I didn't want to force them into anything."

"Aero loves her more than his next breath, doll. The same goes for her. I hear all of the time they're like those books she reads."

I smiled softly. "Yeah, they really are like a romance novel."

"I have to call Winter," Sloane hollered. "Like, right now. I have to tell her everything." Sloane scrambled off the floor and shoved the ring on her finger.

"That the author she's friends with?" Throttle asked.

I nodded. "The one and only. I swear she is going to write a book about Aero and Sloane."

"Odd," Throttle mumbled.

It was, but it was also sweet.

There weren't many real-life love stories that could rival a romance novel. Sloane was lucky to have found Aero, and the whole world needed to know just how great they were together.

"Hold up," Yarder called. "Before you go running out of here, we gotta talk. I'm picking up what you are laying down, but let me just hear it straight."

Throttle elbowed me. "This is your show, doll."

"Oh, uh." I cleared my throat and sat forward. "It's pretty simple. Aero and Sloane are going to run off to get married."

"You're coming with," Sloane interrupted. "It was your idea, and I can't get married without my best friend as my bridesmaid."

"Uh, well," I stammered. That had kind of been the plan, but honestly, I was still shocked that Aero and Sloane had just gotten engaged.

"You and Throttle go with them. It will be more believable if you two go with it. Witnesses and all that shit," Yarder agreed.

"Okay," I drawled.

"That's gonna take like two days, maybe three, tops," Fade pointed out. "You really think that is going to give us enough time to figure out who blew up the gym and the car crashing into the clubhouse?"

"Honeymoon," I blurted. "We could take off to Vegas or some other place that could be considered a vacation spot and spend a week or so there." Or longer. If we drove wherever we were going, that would take more time, too. "The mountains are pretty this time of year."

"Golden, Colorado," Dad called. "I used to go there with your mother all of the time. It's outside of Denver and in a valley of the Rocky Mountains."

"Uh, well, that would work." Mom loved those trips with Dad. They went there before Dad became obsessed with politics and climbing the ladder.

"This is good," Yarder pondered out loud. "This could work."

"There's one catch, though," Compass called. "The past ten minutes or so needs to happen again, but in front of the cameras. You know they are going to want to see all of that mushy shit."

Yarder shrugged. "The camera crew comes tomorrow; we keep a close eye on them while they are here, and then Aero pops the question in front of the cameras. You guys can work out the rest as long as it ends with you four on the road to Golden, Colorado, by nightfall."

"What about my dad?" I called. We had all been focused on the club, as they should be, but even though my dad was the reason for all of this, he still needed a plan, too.

Dad held up his hands. "Don't worry about me. I'm going back to Dallas and plan just to lay low with all the cases they threw at me. If I stay under the radar and keep my mouth shut, I should be fine."

"You just said you know too much. Are you going to feign a case of amnesia or something?" I demanded. "You drive me crazy, and I can really only take talking to you on holidays, but I still love you, Dad. Stay here," I offered.

"Whoa, whoa," Yarder called.

Dad shook his head. "If I disappear, Dove, they will for sure come looking for me. It was risky for me to come here now. I'm going to go back to Dallas and act like everything is normal. I have a few contacts I can reach out to and try to find out more of what Gibbs and Boone are up to."

"No," I called. "Don't go snooping around anymore, Dad. I thi–."

"Your dad is a grown man, Dove," Yarder interrupted. "If he thinks going back to Dallas is for the best, then that is what he should do."

"I can hire some security, Dove, and nothing will happen," Dad promised. He buttoned his suit and turned to Yarder.

Yard stood and talked quietly to Dad.

I shoved my chair back to stand, but Throttle's hand gripped my shoulder.

"Stay," Throttle commanded.

My eyes connected with his. "He shouldn't be sent back to Dallas with no protection."

"He just said he is going to hire security and act like everything is normal. That sounds like a solid plan to me. Your dad got us into this shit, and thankfully, it sounds like he is going to try to help make it stop."

Dad nodded at Yarder and headed out of the room.

"Let me go, Throttle," I growled.

He stared at me for a second but released his hand.

I jumped out of my chair and chased after my dad.

He was at the front door when I called his name, and he turned on his heel. "I'm sorry, Dove. I didn't mean for any of this to happen. I got too caught up in what I wanted and didn't think about anyone else."

"You've been doing that all of my life," I spat. "You even did it when Mom was alive."

"I've made a lot of mistakes in my life, Dove, and for the first time, I am going to do everything I can to fix them."

"You don't have to do this alone," I pleaded. Hell, I don't even think he knew what he was going to do. Going back to normal and snooping around didn't seem very well thought out.

"Just stay with the Iron Fiends, Dove."

"Dad," I pleaded softly. I hated a lot of the things the man did, but he was still my dad at the end of the day. "Please be careful."

He nodded and turned back to the door. "I'd tell you the same thing, Dove, but I know by the way that man sitting next to you looked at you, nothing will ever touch a hair on your head." He opened the door and disappeared into the dark night.

His words rolled around in my head, and I tried to make sense of them. The way Throttle looked at me?

He always looked annoyed when I was around.

"Dove?" Sloane called. She moved next to me and grabbed my hand. "Are you okay?"

"Uh, well, that might have been the last time I saw my dad alive. He muttered something about the way Throttle looked at me, and my best friend just got engaged because we needed to distract a camera crew." Other than that, yeah, I was okay.

"Yeah," Sloane sighed. "Things get weird really quick around here, don't they?"

I squeezed her hand and sighed. "You're getting married."

I could feel her happiness surge through her.

"All because of you," she gushed.

"Nah, I just gave Aero the opening he had been waiting for. Who knew the man already had a ring and everything?" That had really bowled me over.

"And now, this time tomorrow, we are going to be on a road trip headed to Golden, Colorado, with a camera crew in tow." She stepped back, and a tear streaked down her cheek. "I mean, I could do without the camera crew, but this is pretty crazy, Dove."

Yup, it totally was, though I was more worried about my dad than I was myself.

His words played back in my head. *I know by the way that man sitting next to you looked at you, nothing will ever touch a hair on your head.*

What did my dad see that I hadn't?

Whatever it was, he knew that I was safe with the Iron Fiends.

I just hoped it stayed that way.

*

Chapter Thirteen

Throttle

"Is it weird I was more terrified asking her today than I was last night?"

I slid my shades over my eyes and gazed up at the sky. "Uh, yeah, brother. Last night it was just the club; today, you did that shit for all the world to see."

Aero had asked Sloane to marry him for the second time in front of the club, God, and the world, and she had again said yes. Damn, she had been a hell of an actress, too. If I wouldn't have known better, I would have thought Sloane didn't know it was going to happen.

"You think Yarder is selling it to the producers that the camera crew needs to follow us?" Aero asked.

"Yarder could sell a cape to Superman, Aero. I wouldn't worry about it."

If that camera crew didn't follow us to Golden, Colorado, Yarder would personally shove them into their van and push it down the damn road. The camera crew wasn't going to hang around a second longer than Yarder wanted them to.

Dove and Sloane had headed to their rooms to pack, even though they had packed last night. Right now, we were all acting for the cameras, and I prayed it all looked authentic.

Aero plopped onto the bench next to the front door. "In two days, I am going to be a married man, Throttle."

"Yeah, yeah, you are," I chuckled. "I sure as hell didn't see this curve ball heading our way. I was suspicious of Faye being the reason for shit hitting the fan, but come to find out, it was Dove and her dear old dad."

"You can't be mad at Dove for this, Throttle. Even if Russ hadn't sent her to try and find dirt on us, whoever Boone and Gibbs sent after us would still have come. Hell, it's probably a good thing he talked Dove into being a snitch; otherwise, it would have been too late, and we wouldn't have known trouble was headed our way before he took us down."

Aero was right, but it still annoyed the fuck out of me.

If Dove didn't think we were dirty, she should have told us what was going on.

"It is what it is, brother. Can't go back and change things."

I was sure Dove knew she had fucked up, and she had no clue that her dad was into something so much deeper than he led her to believe.

Still, I was pissed.

Yarder walked out the door and looked around the parking lot. "You're good to go. The camera crew is heading to their hotel to pack up their shit, and you guys will be on the road within the hour."

Hook, line, and sinker. I knew Yarder would make the producers see following us to Colorado was better than sticking around the clubhouse and garage.

"They did give me a bit of hell for covering the cameras for a couple of hours yesterday," Yarder smirked and pulled a cigarette out of his pocket. "Told them must have been a glitch, but they didn't believe me because they had screen grabs of Dice and Pirate with their faces front and center right before they were covered."

"I would pay to see those photos," Aero laughed.

"Oh, I have a feeling everyone will see them eventually," Yarder laughed.

The camera crew walked out of the clubhouse and headed to their van.

"We'll be back in half an hour, Yarder," a redhead woman called.

Yarder nodded and lit his cigarette. "Sounds good, Adalee."

They climbed into their van and headed out of the driveway.

"You learned their names?" I asked.

Yarder shrugged. "We did sign up for this shit, and it's not their fault that the shit is hitting the fan while they are here. They are just doing their job."

"Are you drunk or high?" Aero asked.

Yarder shook his head and blew out a cloud of smoke. "Neither. I'm just trying to take in the joy of knowing my ass won't be followed around by the camera crew for the next seven days."

I wasn't thrilled about being the one taking the brunt of being recorded, but it was what it was. Anything for the Iron Fiends. "As long as you take those seven days to figure out who blew up the gym and what the hell is headed our way."

Yarder nodded. "The first one we are going to make happen. I doubt we are going to be able to find out what is heading our way, but we are going to do everything we can to be prepared for it. Boone and Gibbs may be powerful, but I don't know if they've ever gone up against people like the Iron Fiends. We are clean, but that doesn't mean I don't have connections that aren't."

"Just be careful, brother." Aero stood and clapped Yarder on the back. "I'm gonna go check on the girls. Sloane said she was all packed last night, but she said she was going to check things over. I need to make sure she's ready to hit the road by the time the camera crew gets back."

Aero walked back into the clubhouse.

"You really think we're going to be ready for whatever hell is headed our way?"

Yarder took a long drag off his cigarette and blew out a plume of smoke. "Yeah, Throttle. A bunch of guys in suits aren't going to take us down. Just keep a close eye on Dove while you're gone."

"You worried she's going to flip on us or something?"

Yarder tossed his cigarette on the ground and snubbed it out with the toe of his boot. "Nah, she was clueless as to what her dad was up to. The shitstorm he brought might wind up trying to take her out since she's Russ' daughter."

"She's safe with me."

Yarder nodded. "I know. You look at her the same way Aero looks at Sloane."

"And how is that?" I asked.

"Like you'll die before anything bad happens to her."

*

Chapter Fourteen

Dove

"You can sleep, doll."

I scrubbed my hand down my face and shook my head. "I'm good. You shouldn't have to be the only one awake."

Throttle chuckled. "I'm okay being the only one awake. I'm just glad Sloane fell asleep so we could turn off that book she was listening to."

"You didn't enjoy *The Lord of the Rings*?" I laughed. That was what had made me so sleepy. I knew Sloane read all different kinds of books, but that was one I didn't get. Give me the hot firemen, bikers, or cowboys any day over elves and a bunch of rings.

"Not something I'm into, doll."

Throttle interrupted my thought, and I shifted in my seat.

Speaking of hot bikers.

Throttle didn't seem so irritated with me anymore. He seemed to actually tolerate me, which was surprising because I figured for sure when he found out that I was at the clubhouse to spy on them, the whole club would kick me to the curb.

I was wrong.

Sitting in the passenger seat of the club's van on the way to Colorado was not at all how I saw this day going.

"Well," I yawned. "What are you into?"

"Music," he replied simply.

"Can you be more specific?" I laughed.

"Rock."

I figured. I messed with the radio until a rock station came in clear. I sat back in my seat and was surprised I knew the song playing. "Halestorm."

"Huh? Are you getting delirious on me, Dove? The night is clear."

I rolled my eyes. "The band playing is Halestorm," I clarified. "This is one of my favorite songs by them."

Throttle turned it up and listened.

'Dirty Work' was just a banger I never got tired of. When the chorus hit, you couldn't help but do a little headbang.

The song ended, and I was suddenly amped and not tired.

"Doll," Throttle called.

I turned down the radio and smiled at him expectantly. "Well?"

"Not at all what I thought you would listen to," he confessed, "but good."

I don't know why I was so worried about what Throttle thought of my favorite song, but I was relieved to know that he liked it. "What about you?" I asked. "What is your favorite song?"

He shrugged and changed lanes to go around a slow car. "Anything by Black Veil Brides."

"I only know a couple of songs by them." I pulled up my phone and opened my music app. "I'm going to have to add them to my playlist."

"Because I like them?"

I added all their albums to my playlist and tucked my phone back in my pocket. "I just like music. Maybe if I listen to the music you like, I can figure you out a little bit more."

"Figure me out?" he asked.

Oh boy. I should have left that thought in my head. "Uh, not figure you out, just get to know you more." That was not any better than saying I wanted to figure him out.

"Right," he drawled. "'Wake Up' is a favorite, but I'm not sure what that says about me."

I smirked and laid my head back. "I'll listen to it and report back."

He shook his head and flipped on his blinker.

"Are we finally pulling over?" I asked. When I get my second wind, Throttle decides to call it a night. Of course.

Throttle nodded. "Yeah. It's past midnight, and this is the last hotel for a while." He pulled off the exit and pulled into a motel parking lot.

Sloane and Aero woke up in the back seat, and we stumbled into the front door with the camera crew behind us.

"We were wondering when you guys were going to pull over," Adalee called. "Garett was ready to fall asleep behind the wheel."

"Next time, flash us or something," Sloane muttered. Her eyes widened, and she waved her hand. "Your headlights." It still didn't sound right. "On your car." She moved her hand in front of her chest. "Not these headlights."

"Babe," Aero chuckled. He pressed a kiss to her forehead. She leaned into him, and he wrapped his arms around her.

Man, those two were really in love.

"They only have two rooms," Throttle called.

"Uh, we can take one room if you guys take the other," Garett suggested.

"How many beds?" Adalee asked.

"Two full beds in each," Throttle called.

"Perfect," Sloane slurred. "Show me to my room, Gaston."

Throttle quickly paid for both rooms and handed the camera crew a key. "Second floor. See you in the morning, suckas."

"Where are we?" Aero asked.

Throttle pointed in the opposite direction the camera crew headed. "First floor, room 2."

"Two," Sloane chirped. "Two, two."

Aero put his arm around Sloane's shoulders and walked her behind Throttle. "I think she's getting delirious," he chuckled.

I was pretty damn tired, too. "Uh, what time do you guys plan on getting back on the road?"

Throttle stopped in front of room two and inserted the keycard. He held open the door, and I skirted around him behind Aero and Sloane.

"I call bathroom first." Sloane darted into the bathroom and shut the door behind her.

"Okay," I laughed. I guess it had been a little too long since the last pitstop.

Aero dropped his duffel on the floor and stretched his arms over his head. "What time is checkout?" he asked Throttle.

Throttle scrubbed his hands down his scruffy face. "Uh, eleven."

"Cool. I say we head out at eleven-o-one."

Throttle clicked his tongue and pointed at Aero. "Sounds like a solid plan to me."

Oh, thank god. I was really afraid we were only going to get a couple of hours of sleep before they insisted we get back on the road.

Sloane walked out of the bathroom and faceplanted onto the first bed.

"Uh, I guess that's your bed, huh?" Aero laughed. "You girls can have this one."

Well, that was a relief. I thought for sure I was going to wind up sleeping with Throttle. Though I was so tired that I really wouldn't care either way.

I grabbed my bag and headed into the bathroom. I quickly used the bathroom, threw on a pair of sleep shorts, and brushed my teeth.

I must have been in the bathroom longer than I thought because when I walked out, the lights were out, and the room was illuminated only by the TV.

"Uh, Dove?" Aero called.

I dropped my bag by the door and turned, surprised to see Sloane wrapped around Aero in my bed. "Um, okay?"

"She sprung on him like a rabid monkey and dragged him into bed," Throttle laughed. "He was lying down before either of us knew what the hell was going on."

"He's my biker," Sloane muttered sleepily. "Just sleep with Throttle, Dovey."

"Dovey?" Throttle chuckled. He was lying on the other bed with his back against the headboard.

"She only calls me that when she wants something from me," I muttered.

"Look, I can try to move, but I'm pretty sure she's not letting me go."

I waved my hand at Aero and shuffled over to the other bed. "It's fine." It wasn't like Throttle and I were in our own bed, locked up alone.

We were both grown adults who could sleep in the same bed without it meaning anything. I grabbed the covers and slipped into bed.

Yes, Throttle was right next to me, but this was fine.

Everything was fine.

"Good night, Dovey," Sloane called.

I pulled the covers up to my chin and focused on the TV. "Goodnight."

"I'm getting married tomorrow," she sighed.

Aero chuckled. "Yeah, we are."

I sighed and finally relaxed. Sloane and Aero are getting married tomorrow. Who cared if I was in bed with Throttle?

My best friend was going to marry the man of her dreams, and I got to be there.

Throttle slid further into the bed, and his leg brushed against mine.

"Sorry, doll," he muttered.

"You're fine," I whispered. I glanced over at him from the corner of my eye, and my heart raced.

He was shirtless.

Sweet Jesus.

God was punishing me.

My eyes darted back to the TV, and I tried not to think of the shirtless, handsome Throttle six inches away from me.

Sleep did not come easy, even though I was exhausted.

Three and a half episodes of *The Fresh Prince of Bel-Air,* I finally fell asleep.

My dreams were filled with Sloane running around in a wedding dress with Aero chasing behind her and a shirtless Throttle lying in wait for me while I tried to keep up with Sloane.

Even in my sleep, I couldn't get away from Throttle. Right before I woke up, he finally caught me and showed me *exactly* what his shirtless chest looked like up close.

*

Chapter Fifteen

Throttle

Her arm was draped over my chest, and her head was snuggled into the crook of my neck.

This was nice.

I could count on one hand the number of times I had woken with a woman in my arms, and I would still have four fingers available.

Dove was it.

"Brother," Aero called. "We're gonna go get some breakfast. You want us to bring you anything back?"

I should wake up Dove so we could go with them, but I didn't want her to move just yet. "Uh, just get us whatever you guys get. I'll pay you when I get up."

"Don't sweat it," Aero chuckled. "We'll be back in a little bit."

"Are you sure we should leave them alone?" Sloane whispered as he ushered her out the door.

"You're the one who told me Dove needs to wake up on her own; otherwise, she is going to be cranky all day," Aero reminded her.

"Well, yeah," she muttered.

The door clicked close behind them, and then it was just me and Dove.

I didn't know when it happened, but sometime in the middle of the night, our bodies had intertwined.

Her legs were tangled with mine, and the soft wisp of her breath on my shoulder felt like heaven.

I had known Dove since she and Sloane had wandered into the Iron Fiends world, and now it felt like home having her with me.

She stirred against me, but instead of rolling away, she managed to throw one of her legs over mine and trailed the tip of her nose up my neck.

"I'm glad you caught me," she whispered. Her hand drifted up my chest, and she rubbed her foot up and down my leg.

"Dove," I called.

"Hmm," she hummed. "I like it when you say my name."

Uh, this was unexpected but fucking nice.

"Are you sleeping, doll?" I asked.

"No, I was chasing Sloane and Aero, but you caught me," she purred. "Now, what are you going to do with me?"

Yeah, she was asleep.

"Dove, doll, you gotta wake up," I called.

Her lips trailed kisses across my cheek, and her hand moved to cup my cheek.

"Dove," I called louder.

Her eyes drifted open, and her hand froze. "Throttle?" she whispered.

"You awake, doll?" I asked.

She nodded once. "Uh, yes."

"Really?" If she was awake, why hadn't she jumped out of bed and demanded to know what was going on?

"Really," she whispered.

Okay, that was good she was awake. Maybe she needed a second to get her bearings. "Uh, Aero and Sloane went to get us breakfast."

"Okay."

Something was going to have to give. I needed to either get out of this bed or find out how Dove's dream ended. "You want me to get out of bed?" I asked.

She shook her head. "No."

No.

No?

"Are you sure you're awake, doll?" I asked again.

Her hand moved, but not in the direction I thought it would. She caressed my cheek and trailed her fingers over the few days' worth of stubble. "I like you."

"Uh, I like you, too." I did. Now that everything was out in the open, I did like Dove. I could also admit I really liked her hands and body pressed against me.

"Do you?" she whispered.

"Yes, doll."

She hummed under her breath, and I turned my head to look at her. Our eyes connected, and I saw something I had never seen in Dove's eyes before.

Lust.

Whatever dream Dove had had turned her on, and she was still feeling it. "Keep looking at me like that, Dove, and things are going to happen."

"Things like what?" she asked. She trailed her fingers over my lips, and I pressed a kiss to the soft pad of her finger.

"Things that involve less clothes and a whole hell of a lot of kissing." I wasn't going to beat around the bush. I wanted Dove, and I needed her to know that loud and clear. I wasn't into playing games.

"If we kiss, does it just stay in this bed?" she asked softly. "Or will you kiss me later?"

I knew with just one kiss, Dove would be mine.

There was a protectiveness I felt for her before she even touched me, and now, with her body wrapped around me, I knew we could never go back to what we were.

"I kiss you now, I'm not going to be able to stop. Now and later."

There it was, all out there, and now it was her choice on where this was headed.

Her eyes dropped to my lips and then darted back up. "Okay."

I didn't need another word. I didn't know how long Aero and Sloane were going to be, and I wanted to take advantage of every second we had alone.

Her hands roamed over my body, and I rolled her onto her back. I tossed back the covers, and her eyes heated as she took in my tattoos. "I knew there had to be more than what I could see with your shirt on," she whispered.

My lips claimed hers. Sealing both of our fates.

Her lips were a million times softer than I imagined, and her taste was intoxicating. Her hands trailed up and down my back while I grabbed the hem of her shirt and pulled it over her head.

We both managed to shimmy out of our shorts while our lips never left each other.

"Throttle," she gasped when my lips captured her nipple, and she arched her back. My hand snaked down her body and cupped her pussy. "Please," she pleaded.

My fingers parted the lips of her pussy, and a moan ripped from her mouth. I toyed with the tight bud of her clit, and her legs fell to the side, giving me complete access to her body.

"So fucking hot," I growled.

She reached up and pulled me down. Our lips met, and our tongues danced as I brought her closer and closer to the edge.

"I'm close," she gasped finally. "Oh my god."

My finger swirled around her clit, and her orgasm washed over her. My name ripped from her lips, and she threw her head back. Her body rocked beneath me, and her hips moved side to side as she bathed in the afterglow.

I pressed a kiss to the corner of her mouth, and she wrapped her arm around my neck. "I need you, Throttle," she whispered. Her other hand wrapped around my cock, and a gasp escaped her lips.

"Like what you feel?" I asked.

She raised her head up and looked down at her hand. "Well, yeah, and I also like that it's much bigger than I anticipated."

I pressed a kiss to her lips and pushed her back onto the bed. "I'll take that as a compliment, doll."

I positioned my cock and slowly pushed inside her.

"Oh my god," she moaned. She pressed her hips up, and our bodies fully connected.

She was full of my rock-hard cock.

"Yeah," she gasped. "You are very large, Throttle."

I chuckled and pressed a kiss to her neck. "Hold on, doll. The fun is just beginning."

Our hips collided with each downward thrust.

She cried out my name like a prayer on her lips.

I thrust into her and held myself poised above her. "Tell me you want me," I demanded.

"I want you; I want you," she panted. She clawed at my chest and begged me to go faster.

I doubled down and pounded into her. My balls tightened, and I knew I was only a thrust away from coming.

She shouted my name and braced her hands on the headboard as I slammed into her. Her body rolled, and her pussy gripped me like a vise. I emptied my balls inside her, and she mewled with satisfaction as her orgasm coursed through her.

I collapsed on top of her and gathered her in my arms. I rolled onto my back and tucked her against me. "You good?" I asked.

She laid her hand on my chest and calmed her breathing. "Uh, yeah. Like, real good," she giggled. "I wasn't sure if I would remember how to do that."

"Been that long?" I asked.

"You wouldn't even believe me if I told you how long it's been."

"Well," I drawled. "Your dry spell is over, doll."

She sighed softly and traced her fingers over the cross on my chest. Her finger froze, and she raised her head. "Do you hear that?"

I listened closely. "It sounds like a phone ringing."

"It does, but like far away." The ringing stopped for a second and then started again. "That sounds like my phone," she mused.

I glanced at the bedside table and didn't see her phone. "Uh, where did you leave it?" I asked.

She raised up on her elbow, and the phone got louder. "I'm pretty sure it's in the bed," she giggled. She scrambled up on her knees, and I took in the sight of her tits bouncing as she searched for the phone. "You could help me," she laughed. She tugged the sheet from under me, and the phone bounced next to her knee. "Got you." She grabbed the phone and answered it. "Hello?"

She pursed her lips and looked down at me while she listened.

I reached up to touch her boob, but she swatted my hand away. "Stop it," she hissed.

I propped my arms behind my head and smiled.

"No, I was talking to Throttle. Just get me a breakfast sandwich." She put the speakerphone on and held the phone between us. "What do you want for breakfast? The only place they can find food is at the gas station across the street."

"Coffee," I grunted. And hopefully enough time to go another round with Dove.

"He said coffee, but you should probably get him some substance. I think he needs it."

Now that was bold.

I had told her if she and I happened, it was going to happen again, but I didn't know she was going to put it out there right away.

I was into it.

"Take your time coming back," I called.

Dove's mouth dropped open, and her eyes bugged out. "Throttle," Dove gasped.

"Wait, wait," Sloane gasped. "Did you guys… are you…" The phone was muffled. "I think Dove and Throttle had sex."

"Hell yeah," Aero cheered. "We'll take the long way back to the motel, brother," he called.

"Dove Emery Finley. You and I are going to have a long talk when we get back to the room," Sloane scolded. "I didn't even know you liked Throttle."

I grabbed Dove around the waist and pulled her in for a kiss. "Say goodbye to your friend. I think we need to make sure we actually like each other."

"Oh my god! I'm hanging up now, and we will be back in twenty minutes," Sloane warned.

I grabbed the phone. "Make it thirty." I ended the call and tossed it on the nightstand.

"Throttle," Dove laughed. "We just told Sloane and Aero we had sex."

I pulled her on top of me, and she straddled my waist. "Yeah, sure did. I figure we could just skip over the awkwardness of wanting to rip each other's clothes off all the time but have to act like we don't like each other in front of everyone and just tell them."

"We could have just told them we liked each other."

I pressed a kiss to her lips. "And we're having sex." I then pressed a hot, searing kiss to her lips. "Right now."

"Right now?" she giggled.

I nodded and rolled her onto her back. "Right now."

*

Chapter Sixteen

Dove

"Am I the only one completely confused and surprised?"

Adalee nodded. "Um, you are not alone." Her pen was poised over her clipboard. "I need to gather my thoughts."

"How about we get on the road, and you can work on gathering them while we drive to Golden?" I suggested.

"That's exactly what you looked like at the gas station earlier," Aero chuckled. "Sloane's jaw hit the floor, and she dropped her breakfast sandwich."

Throttle and I were standing next to the van, our hands joined like some circus sideshow that was shocking.

And it felt right.

I don't know how we did it, but we skipped over the awkward stage of hooking up and jumped right into being together.

"You bikers sure do move fast," Garett muttered. "Five days ago, Sloane and Aero weren't even engaged, and now we're on the way to some mountain town over nine hundred miles away so they can elope, and you two are completely mind-blowing." He motioned to me and Throttle. "You couldn't stand each other, and now you're a we. You are now a *we*," he repeated. "How does that even happen? One night in a roach motel, and a *we* walks out."

"Does this make sense to anyone?" Throttle asked.

I patted Throttle's shoulder. "I think Garett is having a hard time wrapping his head around you and me."

"I think he's just surprised at how quickly it happened," Max, the boom operator, specified. "You two actually make sense. We all figured it was going to take at least a season or two before you figured it out. Adalee thought you guys would be like Romeo and Juliet, seeing as who Dove's dad is. The Iron Fiends against the Finley's like the Capulets against the Montagues."

Throttle tipped his head to the side. "Dove's dad?" he asked. "What the hell are you talking about?"

How did Adalee and the crew know about my dad? "You guys have never met my dad."

"I know," Adalee laughed. "All it took was a Google search to find out who your dad is, Dove. It's going to be an amazing storyline when he finds out about you two."

Whoa.

Whoa, whoa, whoa.

I didn't care about my dad knowing about Throttle and me. I had a problem with the reality show knowing. For years, I had worked to separate myself from my dad and have my own life, and now, with the show knowing, I could be thrust back into the political life.

And I'm sure the club didn't want it to be known either, seeing how there was a shitstorm brewing over the club thanks to my dad.

No, thank you.

"We're gonna need you to forget about who Dove's dad is," Aero called. "That shit doesn't go in the show."

Adalee glanced at Garett. "Uh, well, you might need to talk to the producers because I've already told them. They were concerned about our footage being boring, and I mentioned a few storylines we figured would happen." She pointed at Throttle and me. "You two and your dad not liking each other was one we pitched."

"They ate it up like a piece of cake," Max laughed.

I looked up at Throttle.

This was not good.

"Before you guys report back to the producers, let me call Yarder." Aero held up his phone. "Keep your lips sealed until I say so, ya dig?"

Adalee held up her hands. "Fine, fine. But you guys are going to be fighting an uphill battle if you think you are going to be able to bury the fact the state attorney general's daughter is dating someone from the club."

We loaded up into our vehicles and continued onto Golden.

Aero was in the back on the phone with Yarder while Sloane was leaning in between the front seats.

"How did the camera crew call you two hooking up, and I had zero clue?" she demanded. "I'm the best friend and should know everything before anyone else." She bumped Throttle's shoulder. "You included. You sneak in under the radar and sweep Dove off her feet without a sound."

Throttle glanced at me. "I don't know if I would say I swept her off her feet. She was the one who climbed me like a tree in her sleep."

"You let me," I muttered.

"I have so many questions," Sloane muttered.

"I'll tell you whatever you want to know as long as you don't report it all back to Winter." Sloane's life could be an open book for Winter, but I wasn't too hyped on mine being fodder for a book.

Sloane threw up her hands and sat back. "Whatever. I'm just happy in a few short hours, I will be married and my best friend found her own biker."

I glanced at Throttle to see if he had any reaction to Sloane calling him my biker. "My Romeo," I laughed. "At least according to the camera crew, he's my Romeo."

Throttle grabbed my hand and pressed a kiss to the back of it. "Let's just hope we have a better ending than they did."

Wasn't that the truth?

*

Chapter Seventeen

Throttle

"That was fucking easy."

Sloane waved the piece of paper in the air. "We've got our marriage license," she cheered.

"And it's fucking crazy that you guys could sign that right now, and you're officially married," Dove mused. "Like, you guys don't need an officiant or even witnesses."

Apparently, Colorado was one of the easiest states in America to get married. Hell, there was literally a ten-minute wait to get the license.

We had been in Golden for a total of thirty minutes, and Sloane had her marriage license in hand.

The camera crew moved around us, and people near us were taking notice. I didn't think Golden was the type of town that was used to a camera crew filming. Especially not two bikers and their ol' ladies.

That was still crazy to think about.

I had an ol' lady.

"Excuse me."

I turned and pulled Dove into my arms to make way for a woman coming down the sidewalk.

The woman stopped in front of us and put her hands on her hips.

"Hi?" Dove asked.

The woman smiled wide. "Hi," she chirped. "I saw you guys when you came into town."

She seemed harmless, but Aero and I were on alert in case this chick was someone who was going to try to hurt us.

"In the van?" Sloane asked. "I know it's a creeper van, but I didn't think it was that noticeable."

"No," the woman laughed. "I meant when you guys were walking down Main Street. I actually noticed your guys' cuts first."

The hairs on the back of my neck stood up.

The woman thrust her hand out to Dove. "I'm Hannah. My fiancé is part of an MC in town. I'm so used to seeing VII Knights cuts that I was shocked to see a different MC."

Oh.

Oh fuck.

We were in a town that had an MC, and here we were, walking around their town with a camera crew like we owned the place. We very well might be in a town where the local MC did not appreciate having other clubs just appear.

Dove shook her hand and glanced at me. "Uh, we're just in town for a couple of days. My parents used to come here years ago, and my friends decided to come here to get married."

Probably a little bit more information than I would have given, but it was fine.

Sloane was still holding the marriage license, and obviously, we weren't from around here.

Hannah's eyes bugged out. "You're getting married here? Where? Did you book the church?"

Sloane shook her head. "Uh, actually, we don't know where we are getting married. Aero asked me suddenly, and I didn't want to wait. Dove's dad mentioned this place, and here we are."

"Seriously?" Hannah asked.

There was a good possibility she thought we were all idiots.

"Uh, yeah." Sloane hooked her arm through Aero's. "Like I said, this is all really sudden."

"Where are you guys from?" Hannah asked.

"Texas," I replied. "We're not trying to step on anyone's toes by being here."

Hannah reared back. "You guys are totally welcome here. The club would love to meet you guys."

Dove glanced at me.

Hannah pulled out her phone. "Let me see what Ice is up to today." She smiled wide, pressed a few buttons, and put her phone to her ear. "The club owns

Knight Building, and I never know where they are."
She pasted a cheery smile on her face and waited.

Aero turned his head toward me so Hannah couldn't hear him. "I don't know how to feel about this shit, brother. Part of me is on alert with her being so nice to us, but then I know Sloane would do the same damn thing if the tables were turned."

"Same," I muttered. "Just stay alert, and we'll see how this goes."

"Ice?" Hannah called. "It's me. I'm in town, and I happened to make some new friends." She paused a bit and then continued. "They're from Texas and part of an MC. Wouldn't it be fun to invite them to the clubhouse?"

Aero glanced at me. "I'm picturing Yarder on the other end of that phone and all the cuss words he would be saying."

"Uh, I'm in front of Bay Books, why?" Hannah called.

"Uh, oh," I muttered.

Hannah turned and looked down the street. "Okay." She ended the call and smiled brightly. "Ice and Mercury are actually just down the street. They're on the way."

Jesus.

A blacked-out truck rolled down the street and parked across the street.

"Honey," Hannah called.

The driver opened his door, and a large brown dog jumped down. He barreled across the street and straight into Hannah.

"God dammit, Samson," the man called. "Can you at least look when you cross the street?"

"Daddy took you to work today, didn't he?" Hannah cooed to the dog.

Sloane crouched down next to Hannah and meekly petted Samson.

I watched the man cross the street, but my eyes moved to the man who got out of the passenger seat.

"Fifty bucks says he's the prez," Aero muttered.

I was not going to bet against that.

The two men made it across the street and stood behind Hannah.

Hannah stood, and the driver of the truck pulled her into his arms.

The passenger nodded to Aero and me. "I'm Mercury, prez of the VII Knights MC."

The other man raised his hand. "I'm Ice." He reached out his hand to Aero. "Nice to meet you guys."

"Aero."

I tipped my head to them. "I'm Throttle, and this is Dove."

Aero nodded to Sloane, who was still petting the dog. "And that is Sloane."

"And they are getting married," Hannah cheered. "Here! They just got their license and were trying to figure out where to do it."

Mercury nodded. "Congrats."

"There's a chapel down by the river," Ice offered.

"Oh," Hannah sighed. "That place is so pretty. It's a tiny steepled church that the river runs behind."

Sloane looked up expectantly at Aero. "That sounds really nice."

Aero shrugged. "I don't care where we do it as long as you sign that paper, babe."

"Look, honey," Hannah laughed. "He's as romantic as you are. It must be a biker thing."

Ice scoffed.

Sloane stood and moved next to Aero. "Uh, do you know who we can contact about getting married at the church? I know we could technically just sign this paper and be married, but I wanted some kind of a ceremony."

"I do!"

Sloane waited for Hannah to tell her who owned it.

Hannah excitedly pointed her finger into her chest. "I own it. I bought it last summer since it butts up to our house. I'm kind of modest about telling people about it, and Ice picked up right away that someone needed to tell you guys about it, but it wasn't going to be me."

Ice rolled his eyes. "Tell me how someone who owns the huge sawmill in town can be modest."

Hannah now rolled her eyes. "My sister basically owns it, and I'm the company accountant." She waved her hand. "But that's not important. What is important is you guys are getting married, and you can totally use my chapel if you want!"

"I, uh." Sloane glanced at Aero.

Aero shrugged. "If that's what you want, babe."

Sloane turned to Dove.

"Uh, duh. You totally need to get married at the chapel with the river running behind it," Dove laughed. "You'd be crazy not to."

Sloane clapped her hands together. "Then it's decided. We would love to get married at your chapel."

Hannah pumped her fist in the air. "Yes! And I know just the person to marry you." She pointed at Mercury, who just rolled his eyes but didn't protest. "Mercury has married nine other couples in town, and you guys would make ten. However, we might have to push back the big day to tomorrow so I can do a little cleaning and decorating. Is that okay?"

Sloane nodded and threaded her fingers through Aero's. "Tomorrow is perfect."

Dove sheepishly raised her hand. "You wouldn't happen to also know of a place to stay, would you?"

Hannah beamed proudly. "There just so happens to be a three-bedroom cottage set back from the chapel that was the minister's home when there were Sunday services."

"Oh, uh, I was more talking about a hotel or something. You're already doing so much for us by letting us use the chapel." Dove tipped her head down the street. "We're not picky."

"Nonsense. It's perfect for you to stay at the cottage. It's all ready for visitors. Just give me an hour to make sure everything is perfect, and you guys can head down there."

Dove glanced at me.

"Whatever you guys want, doll." It wasn't like we had a real plan for what we were going to do once we got to Golden.

"We'll take it," Sloane chirped. "We'll totally take you up on the offer to stay in a three-bedroom cottage just feet away from your white chapel where Aero and I will get married."

Hannah, Ice, Mercury, and Samson took off after Hannah rattled off her phone number and the address to the chapel and cottage and asked us to give her an hour before we dropped in.

We watched the black truck drive away, and I noticed Garett off to my side.

He lowered the camera and shook his head. "That right there is what I am talking about. I don't know how it happens, but shit happens so quickly around you guys. You went from having no clue where to get married to finding a chapel down by the river with a three-bedroom cottage the perfect size for all of us. I won't even get into the fact that they are being married by the prez of a local MC." Garett shook his head and raised the camera. "Fucking wild, man."

I was starting to see what Garett was talking about. That was an eventful first hour in Golden. Who knew what the next seven days would have in store for us?

*

Chapter Eighteen

Dove

"I'm getting married."

I curled the last section of my hair and set the curling iron on the edge of the sink. "Yes."

"Today."

I looked at Sloane in the mirror and nodded. "Yes."

"To Aero," Sloane clarified.

"Again, yes." I was pretty sure Sloane was just trying to sike herself up, but I figured it didn't hurt for me to chime in.

Hannah had tucked us away in a room in the back of the chapel while Aero and Throttle had stayed in the cottage to get ready.

Garett and the crew had been going back and forth between the two places getting footage for the show, but Adalee had stayed with us as she used her small camera to get still shots of the chapel, Sloane, and me.

"This is crazy." Sloane waved her hand in her face and plopped down on the closed toilet. "I'm crazy."

Oh, boy. At first, I thought Sloane was just excited, but now she might be on the brink of a freakout.

Adalee appeared in the doorway of the bathroom, looking at her camera. "This place is magical. You guys need to see these shots I just got. When this episode airs, Golden is going to be overrun with people wanting to have their own biker wedding on the river."

Sloane looked around frantically and bared her teeth as she struggled to breathe. "Oh my god," she wheezed.

I crouched down in front of Sloane and grabbed her hands. "You gotta breathe, babe, okay? This is the best day of your life, yeah? Hee, hee, whoo, just breathe with me. Hee, hee, whoo."

"Hee, hee, whoo," Sloane mimicked. "Hee, hee, whoo."

"Oh, god," Adalee called. "Is she going to be okay? Isn't that how you're supposed to breathe through contractions?"

I nodded and patted Sloane's hands. "She is perfect. And who says you can only breathe like this if you're having a baby? Breathing in general right now is good."

"I'm getting married," Sloane wheezed. She looked at Adalee. "I'm getting married to my biker in a chapel on the river with my best friend, the guy she's sleeping with, and a camera crew for a reality TV show." She sucked in a frantic breath. "Oh my god."

Okay, something needed to distract Sloane. "Have you talked to Winter?" I asked.

Sloane shook her head. "No."

"Do you want to?" I pulled out my phone. "We could call her right now. She would absolutely flip when you tell her what we're going."

"Yeah, yeah," Adalee agreed. "Let's give her a call."

Sloane nodded and rattled off her number. "She's going to think I'm insane."

I entered the number and connected the call. "Uh, no, girl. Your romance author friend is going to think this is the most amazing thing. Ever."

"Hello?" Winter called.

"Winter," Sloane wheezed.

"Sloane?" she asked, concerned. "Are you okay?"

Sloane waved her hand at me. "Hee, hee, whoo," she breathed out.

"Uh, hey, Winter," I called. "It's Dove, Sloane's best friend."

"Oh, uh, hey. Is everything okay? Is that Sloane breathing weird?"

I couldn't help but laugh. "Uh, yes, that is Sloane."

"She's not having a baby," Adalee called. "She's just having a panic attack."

"Oh, uh, okay," Winter laughed nervously.

"I'm getting married," Sloane blurted. "I'm getting married in a beautiful little white chapel that Hannah owns on the river. I'm getting married to Aero while Dove, Throttle, and the camera crew watch. My pastor, but not a pastor, is the prez of the local MC. I'm getting married," she repeated. "Holy cow."

"What?" Winter shrieked. "You're getting married today?"

Sloane nodded. "Hee, hee, whoo."

"Uh, she's nodding her head, Winter," I explained. "This sort of happened quickly, and I think it's hitting Sloane that it's happening. I thought maybe you might have some of those encouraging romantic words Sloane says you are so good at."

"Oh, uh, well," Winter hemmed. "Like right now, you need words?" She mumbled under her breath, and the phone rustled. "Words are hard."

Oh boy.

Sloane let out a giggle.

"Speaken words are hard. Spoken," she corrected herself. "Spoken words are hard. My god,"

Winter wheezed. "Maybe I could send her an email she could read."

Maybe this wasn't the best idea. We didn't have time for an email. "I'm sure she would love an email from you later, but right now, I need some spoken words." A giggle escaped my lips, and I slapped my hand over my mouth.

"I love love," Winter called. "I love the love Sloane and Aero have. It's one of the few times I've ever seen a man look at a woman the way I write it. He has a twinkle in his eye and a glow that radiates off of him whenever she is near. I don't know how you managed to get in a chapel down by the river, much better than a van by the river, am I right?" she rambled. "Focus, Winter," she told herself out loud. "But I know that's where you are meant to be, Sloane. I know Aero is your biker, and you can't let that go because he's not going to let you go."

"My biker," Sloane sighed. "I got my biker."

"Yes, girl," Winter called. "You got your biker, and now you are going to make it official official by marrying him in a little white chapel surrounded by all of your friends and family."

Winter must have missed the part where she rattled off it was just me, Throttle, and a camera crew. Details.

"I'm getting married," Sloane said again, but this time it wasn't as panicked. "I'm getting married to my biker."

"Hallelujah," Winter laughed. "Say it again, girl."

"I'm getting married to my biker!" Sloane stood and pumped her fist in the air. "I'm marrying my book boyfriend, and I am going to have the best sex of my life for the rest of my life."

Well, Sloane didn't have to throw that out there, but whatever was going to help get her down the aisle.

"Yeah, to amazing sex for the rest of your life," Adalee cheered.

"Let's do this!" Sloane grabbed the phone from me. "Thank you, Winter. I love you, and I promise I'll call you when we get back home."

"Uh, girl, you better because I get the gist of what you are up to, but I have a million and one questions. Good luck, and go get your biker, babe."

Winter ended the call, and Sloane handed me my phone.

Her eyes connected with mine, and finally saw my best friend staring back at me. "I'm getting married."

*

Chapter Nineteen

Throttle

"Once all this bullshit is behind us, Sloane and I are doing this again, but back home."

I drained my beer and crushed it. "Okay?" Their wedding today seemed pretty fucking perfect to me. I didn't know why he wanted to do it again.

Aero and I were on the back deck of the cottage, leaning against the railing with the sun setting in front of us. "Don't get me wrong, man, today was perfect, but it would have been even better to have my brothers and family surrounding us."

"You weren't a fan of Mercury being the officiant and Ice in the back consoling Hannah while she cried?" I chuckled. "I've never seen a chick cry so much when she's happy." Hannah had said she was going to invite the whole club but decided it probably wasn't the best to have a room full of people we didn't know watch Aero and Sloane marry.

"Yeah," Aero sighed. "Thank god Dove and Sloane aren't criers."

"Why not have a big ass party to celebrate?" I suggested. "People do that, don't they? When I was in high school, I had a friend whose sister ran off to

Hawaii or some shit to get married, and when they got back, they had a big ol' party. It was a fucking amazing party, too."

Aero nodded and tipped his head to the side. "That would work. And you and I both know the Iron Fiends know how to throw a party."

That we did. "But you might want to discuss this with Sloane, seeing as you married her," I advised.

"Shut up," Aero chuckled. "And I plan on running it by her."

My phone buzzed in my pocket, and I pulled it out to see Head Dick on the screen.

"You know Yarder is going to kick your ass if he ever sees what you have him saved as in your phone," Aero chuckled.

I shrugged and connected the call to speaker. "Hello?"

"Did she actually say yes, or is Aero crying in his beer?" Yarder asked.

"Fuck you," Aero called. "She said yes."

"Good, good," Yarder laughed. "She must not be as smart as I thought if she actually went through with it."

"You got a reason for calling other than giving me shit on my wedding day?" Aero grunted.

"Got a wedding present for you. Actually, a present for both of you."

I tipped my head to the side. "I didn't get married, Yarder."

"Yeah, yeah, not yet. I give it a month before you're headed down the aisle just like Aero." Yarder chuckled. "Cue Ball might beat you to it first."

"Uh, what?" I asked.

"Don't play stupid, Throttle. I do talk to Aero when you aren't around."

"You bastard," I growled at Aero. I was going to tell Yarder about me and Dove, but I hadn't had the time yet. It's not like it was going to matter what Yarder thought about it.

Aero shrugged. "It wasn't like you guys were hiding it. The whole cottage could hear you two in the shower this morning." Aero tipped his head to the side. "The camera crew, too. Yarder needed a heads-up about what was going on. It's probably for the best anyway, so now you and Dove can be the ones distracting the camera crew."

"Dove's dad being the state attorney general is probably going to help with that," Yarder growled. "I don't know how the hell that one is going to play out on TV, but there isn't much we can do about it now."

"He told you about that, too, huh?" I cringed.

"Yeah, I should have known the show would do a deep dive on everyone, Dove included." Yarder cleared his throat. "But that's not why I'm calling."

"Spit it out, Yarder. I've only got about two minutes before Sloane comes out here looking for me. We got dinner reservations at a place in town."

"We know who blew up the gym."

Aero and I were both speechless.

"Faye's ex. The douche was pissed she was moving on from him and decided he would blow her up," Yarder explained.

"Her ex who cheated on her all the time and also hit her?" Aero asked. "What a fucking whack job."

"Yeah, well, he managed to stay off our radar for this long, so he's not stupid. We're assuming he didn't know Olive had switched shifts with Faye the night he blew up the gym, and he also didn't consider that he was fucking with the Iron Fiends by blowing up one of our sources of income."

"So you guys grab him?" I asked.

"Working on it," Yarder grunted. "Compass has a lead on him and took Fade and Dice to grab him."

"Let us know when they get him," I called.

"Will do. Congrats on getting Sloane to marry you before she realized you're a tool," Yarder laughed. "Make sure you play it up for the cameras so they keep off my ass back here."

"Happy to take one for the club," Aero smiled.

"Have fun, but stay safe. We may have figured out who blew up the gym, but Boone and Gibbs are still on our asses."

"Haven't figured out any more about that?" I asked. Part of me wished the gym and car driving into the clubhouse were connected just so we didn't have two targets on our backs.

"Nothing. We're just watching our backs and laying low. No one in the clubhouse, and even in the garage, we're being extra careful. You guys do the same. Trust no one." Yarder ended the call, and I shoved my phone into my pocket.

"Good news for a good day," Aero sighed.

I nodded. "That it is."

"Aero," Sloane called. "Are you ready to go?" She appeared at the screened-in back door and leaned against the doorframe. "The camera crew is ready. Our reservation is for seven, but they need some time to set up and get the lighting right."

"How the hell did our lives get to having to worry about the camera crew having good lighting?" Aero chuckled. He pumped his fist against mine and headed into the house. "Later, brother."

"Be careful and have fun," I called.

Dove walked out of the cottage and moved next to me. "And then there were two."

I smirked and put my arm around her shoulders. "You hungry? I saw a bar in town claiming they served the best burger in Golden."

She quirked her eyebrow. "I am hungry, but not for food."

"Doll," I groaned. "At least let me feed you before you jump my bones." I turned and rested my hip on the rail. I grabbed Dove around the waist and pulled her into my arms.

"If you want to feed me, then this might not be the best move," she giggled.

I pressed a kiss to her lips and palmed her ass. "Maybe we can see if they deliver."

*

Chapter Twenty

Dove

"You gotta stop that."

"Stop what?" I purred. I rolled into Throttle and draped my arm over his chest.

"That hip roll. Fucking hell, woman. I thought I saw stars," Throttle growled.

I knew he had wanted to take me out to eat, but I had other plans in mind. Thankfully, the bar had delivery, and we managed to scarf down the best burger I had ever had between rounds one and two.

I trailed my fingers down his chest and laid my head on his shoulder. "I'm glad you liked that."

"I like everything you do, doll."

A sigh escaped my lips. "Right back at you, Throttle. You sort of annoyed me for a bit, but now even you breathing turns me on."

"Glad you like me breathing," he chuckled.

I slapped his chest. "Don't make fun of me. This is the best day I have had in a long time, and I want it to stay that way. My best friend married the perfect man for her in this amazing place, and you guys figured out who blew up the gym. There aren't many ways this day could get better."

"You naked in my arms is going to make every day perfect. We should come back here when we're ready to–." Throttle's words died in his throat, and I tipped my head back to look at him.

"Were you going to say we should come back here when we're ready to get married?"

Throttle's eyes darted side to side. "Uh, well."

"Because I would really like that, though I think I would need more people with us. I'm sure Sloane wouldn't change anything about today because she got to marry Aero, but having the club here would have given this day five stars."

"Doll," he drawled.

"Yes, Throttle. I knew what you were going to say, and it doesn't scare me. Sure, we just got together, but don't most people who get into relationships hope they are going to end in marriage? At least for a bit?" I rambled. "Though the thought of marriage was fleeting in all of my relationships. Most of the time, I tried to picture myself walking down the aisle toward them, and I just couldn't see it. Hell, most of the time, I laughed at the thought. Coming back to Golden to get married is a great one because even though I don't like my dad some days, I would want him with me when we get married because he came here with my mom when I was younger, and that makes me feel like she would approve of coming here to marry you." I needed to shut up. I was just trying to explain to Throttle that marriage wasn't terrifying. Especially not with him. "I'm rambling." The best way to stop rambling was to announce you were rambling. "Sorry."

Throttle pressed a kiss to my lips. "I think you said it perfectly, Dove. We both are heading in the same direction, and that is back to Golden one day."

A soft smile played on my lips. "Did we just skip over another stage of dating?"

"Probably, but it's not like I'm going to ask you to marry me right now, right?" he winked and tossed back the covers. "The cameras aren't even around."

*

Chapter Twenty-One

Throttle

"The amount of footage we got from the drive to Golden, the wedding, hanging around Golden, and then the road trip back to Mt. Pleasant is insane. Vic and Nancy are going to go crazy when they see everything."

I grunted and hooked the gas pump back. "You can thank Sloane and Dove for the long-ass road trip back." I rubbed the back of my neck and was beyond happy to know we would be back in Mt. Pleasant by nightfall and in my own bed.

"This is by far the best job I have ever had." Garett shook his head. "My last shoot was for one of those housewives shows, and man, it was not fun."

I had no clue what Garett was talking about, and I wasn't sure I liked that he had gotten chattier with me on this trip. It was harder to ignore the cameras when I knew the faces behind them.

The road trip he was so excited about involved Great Sand Dunes National Park, Million Dollar Highway, two places that were in cooking shows Sloane watched, six Buc-ee's, and ten other places I couldn't remember because it all just became a blur after day two.

"I love this place!" Sloane shouted. She thrust a huge red cup with a beaver on it in the air and twirled around. "Everyone should go to Buc-ee's on their honeymoon."

Make that seven Buc-ee's.

"Yeah," Aero drawled behind her. "Buc-ee's is right up there for places want to honeymoon." He grabbed Sloane's hand and pulled her into his arms.

Dove trailed behind them with two plastic bags dangling from her hand and a pillow under her arm. "I got a new pillow for my bed." She held up the bright red pillow that had a beaver in the middle of it.

"Nice, doll," I laughed. It was a good thing there wasn't a Buc-ee's close to Mt. Pleasant because Sloane and Dove would live there.

Everyone piled back into their vehicles, and I cranked up the van.

"How many hours until we're home?" Sloane asked.

"Two hours until we are back in Mt. Pleasant and on lockdown in the clubhouse," Aero drawled.

Dove wrinkled her nose. "You could have left that last part out," she grumbled. "You just ruined my Buc-ee's buzz."

"Well, you better hold on to that buzz, doll, because this is the last Buc-ee's on our trip." I pulled out of the parking lot and back onto the freeway.

"Totally killing my Buc-ee's buzz." She reached into one of the bags and pulled out a stuffed beaver. "Thankfully, this guy will help."

"My god, Dove," I laughed.

"I got the same one!" Sloane laughed. "It's my last souvenir of the best trip ever."

"Awe," Dove sighed. "That's why I got him, too. This really was the best time ever. It's crazy to think we're heading back into the shitstorm my dad created."

I reached over and threaded my fingers through Dove's. "None of this is your fault, doll."

"Even though I agreed to spy on you guys?" she mused.

"Even that," Sloane called, "because you knew you weren't going to find any dirt on the Iron Fiends and were just doing what you could to get your trust fund."

I didn't want Dove to feel that any of what was happening with dad was her fault. There was no way she could have known what a shitstorm he was stirring up. Hell, her dad didn't know what the hell he had been getting into.

Sure, it would have been better if Dove had come to the club right away about what her dad wanted her to do, but we couldn't do back.

The only thing we could do was go forward, and Dove was going to be by my side the whole time.

*

Dove

I didn't even want to think about my trust fund. God knew what was going to happen to it. I assumed my dad would keep control of it to keep me under his thumb, though he should be throwing it at me since he so royally fucked everything up.

"Thank god you still don't think I'm a rat." That had sucked big time when the club and Throttle thought I was some spy trying to get them in trouble.

"For the record, even when I thought you were a rat, I also thought you were hot." Throttle winked at me.

I rolled my eyes and laid my head on the seat. "Thank you, I think."

A sign for Mt. Pleasant was on the side of the road, and it was like a cup of cold water dumped over me.

Our week-long adventure of distracting the camera crew was over, and it was time to get back to our real reality.

*

Chapter Twenty-Two

Throttle

"You, too, huh?"

I threw back the shot Dice placed in front of me.

"Dropping like fucking flies," Pirate muttered.

"You'd drop too if Dove looked your way." I wiped my mouth with the back of my hand and nodded to Dice for a refill.

"Well, yeah," Pirate grumbled, "but I really didn't think you would be next. I mean, you're the biggest son of a bitch next to Yarder."

"I think we're all sons of bitches, Pirate," I chuckled. "I was just lucky enough to find the one woman who's willing to put up with me for longer than one night."

"But what if I like the one night?" Pirate asked. "It's gotta be boring after a while to be with the same person day in and out."

"Ask me in twenty years, brother. I'll let you know." I tossed back the shot and grimaced. "I'm still a son of a bitch, but now I'm a lucky one."

*

Chapter Twenty-Three

Dove

"I'm so happy for you, but I also hate you." Olive flopped back on Sloane's bed next to me and threw her hands over her head. "I have never been so bored in my life. Faye barely came out of her room, and every time I so much as got close to the edge of the driveway, Cue Ball or one of the guys would holler at me and drag me back inside."

"At least you were trapped here with Cue Ball," I offered.

Olive raised her middle finger in the air. "Wrong," she droned. "I was trapped here with Cue Ball, seven men, and my ten-year-old son. I'm not even going to include Faye because I only need two fingers to count how many times she willingly talked to me. As soon as she found out it was her douchebag ex who had tried to blow up me and the gym, she just beats herself up for everything."

Sloane finished zipping up her suitcase and tucked it under the bed. "None of that was her fault."

"I know," Olive moaned. "It's Faye who can't seem to get that, and I get how she can't get that. The last time I talked to her, she was beating herself up for even dating Anthony. That was a long, shitty relationship that fucked with her head. Hell, Fade was nice to her, and she went off the deep end trying to love bomb him but just drove him away."

"Why don't we all go try to talk to her?" I suggested. "Maybe if she hears from all of us that the explosion wasn't her fault, it might sink in a little bit." I knew Faye was dealing with a lot of trauma and guilt, but it wouldn't hurt to let her know that we were all here for her. I hadn't spent much time with Faye, but I liked the time I had spent with her.

I pulled Olive off the bed and grabbed Sloane's hand. "Let's go."

We made the short walk to Faye's room, and I raised my hand to knock.

"Faye," Olive called. "Sloane and Dove are home. I need you to be on my side of being annoyed they got to have all of the fun while we had to stay here."

I tipped my head to the side and knocked again. "Faye?" I called.

Sloane bumped me out of the way and opened her door.

"I'd say we're invading her privacy by opening the door, but she's not even in here," Olive grumbled.

Faye's room looked like all the others. Bed, dresser, and a bathroom. She did have a yellow blanket draped at the foot of her bed, and the top of her dresser was littered with empty soda cans and candy wrappers.

Olive held up a wrapper. "See, I should be in here eating with her."

I rolled my eyes and backed out of her room. "Maybe she went to the kitchen," I pondered.

We made our way into the common room, looking for Faye, but didn't find her anywhere.

"Uh, well," Sloane muttered. "This is not good, but I don't want to raise the alarm because I don't want the guys yelling at her for not being in the clubhouse."

"She has to be here," Olive muttered. "Let's check the garage." I wasn't sure why Faye would be in the garage, but it was worth a look.

"Where you going?" Throttle called. He was at the bar with Dice and Pirate, doing shots in the middle of the day.

I waved my hand at him. "To the garage. No need to get all macho on us."

"Just you, doll," he called. "You're the only one I want to be macho on."

I tipped my head to the side. "I don't know how, but that turned me on." I was pretty sure the man could read me the phone book, and I would want to rip his clothes off by the time he got to the b's.

"Dove," Sloane hissed. "You need to focus and not on your biker."

I shrugged and headed toward the front door. "He's not my biker." I glanced over my shoulder at him and laughed. "He's my Romeo."

"Gag," Olive laughed.

"Hey, didn't you tell me Cue Ball was your savior?" Sloane laughed. "It seems like we all found what we needed."

"Well, I mean, Cue Ball was my savior. It's fitting," she mumbled defensively.

I led the way to the garage and ducked into the front office.

"What the hell are you three doing here?" Yarder called from his office.

"Of course, they have a bell over the door," I grumbled.

"Uh, we're just looking for Faye," Olive called. "Have you seen her?"

"I thought we were trying to keep it under wraps that we can't find Faye?" Sloane whispered.

Yarder moved to the doorway of his office. "She's in the parts storeroom. I don't know why, but she hangs out in there a lot."

"And you let her?" I asked.

He shrugged. "If I let her in there, I know where she is. One less we need to keep an eye on." He raised his eyebrow. "Speaking of, anyone know you three headed out here."

I hitched my thumb toward the clubhouse. "We told Throttle, Dice, and Pirate we were coming here."

He looked around us. "And one of them didn't follow?"

Uh, oh. We might have just gotten the guys in trouble.

"It's a short walk," Sloane reasoned. "We are more than capable of getting here on our own."

Yarder tipped his head to the side but didn't say anything.

"But it doesn't matter how short of a walk it is," Olive droned. "Someone should be with us if we step outside the clubhouse." Olive rolled her eyes and motioned to Yarder. "This is what I had to deal with for a week while you guys were gallivanting all over the country getting married."

"You had to deal with the club doing everything to keep you safe. Fucking rude of us." Yarder pointed to an open door. "Head that way, and then take a left. First door on the left is where you'll find Faye." He slammed his office door shut, and I felt slightly bad about being annoyed with the club protecting us.

Only slightly, though.

We headed down the hallway, took a left, and opened the first door on the left.

"Faye?" Olive called. "Are you in here, honey?"

The room had racks lining the walls and a row of them down the middle. They were organized with signs in front of each box labeling what they were.

"This is oddly satisfying," Sloane called. She trailed her fingers over a row of boxes. "Who knew the guys could actually be neat and orderly about something?"

"I did it," Faye called. "I'm assuming that's why Yarder lets me hang out in here." She was seated on the floor against the back row of shelving. "They had it somewhat organized, but I've made it ten times better. I figured it was the least I could do."

Olive moved to Faye and sank down on the floor next to her. "Least you could do for what?" I asked. I had a feeling I knew what she was going to say but hoped I was wrong.

"For everything," Faye whispered. "If I hadn't been so stupid to keep going back to Anthony, none of this would have happened. The gym wouldn't have exploded with Olive inside it."

"I wasn't inside it," Olive pointed out, "and that wasn't your fault. Anthony is the only one who is going to pay for that."

"If it wasn't for me, Anthony wouldn't have had a reason to blow up the gym, Olive. Your reasons and excuses aren't valid."

"If I wouldn't have been born, my dad wouldn't have targeted the Iron Fiends in his scheme to become US attorney general and then get screwed over by the bad dudes who were helping him," I offered. I wasn't trying to be one up on her, but to show her we all had things done to and around us that we couldn't stop.

"Then why aren't you sitting in the storeroom with me every day?" Faye laughed.

Olive put her arm around Faye's shoulder and pulled her in for a hug. "You can be sad and mad about what happened, Faye, but you can't push me away." She nodded to Sloane and me. "You can't push any of us away."

"Sometimes I just don't feel like talking, Olive. I come in here because nothing demands I be happy or tell them what's wrong." Faye leaned her head back and closed her eyes.

"Then we'll just sit with you. We don't need always to talk," Sloane offered. "Hell, this place is pretty peaceful. I'll need to remember to come here when I want a place to read."

Faye smiled and opened her eyes. "I'm sorry, guys. I just feel bad about what happened, and then I totally messed things up with Fade. I didn't want to be a sad sack you guys had to worry about."

Olive squeezed her shoulder. "Faye, I'm only going to say this once, and you better remember it. We don't care if you're mad, sad, happy, or crazy. We will always be here for you. Nothing can stop us from caring about you."

"Even if I keep making the stupidest mistakes like going back again and again to a piece of a shit man until he tries to blow me up?" Faye laughed.

"You only get one more pass on that one, Faye. I'm hopeful you won't do that ever again." Olive pressed a kiss to the side of her head. "You are worth so much more than how Anthony treated you. Don't ever forget that."

"Fine," Faye sighed. "But I reserve the right to come here when I need to be alone."

"Only if I'm not here with a good book first," Sloane muttered.

I elbowed her in the side. "Stop."

Sloane rolled her eyes. "She can't have all the good hiding places."

"You just got married, Sloane. I don't think you would already need to be hiding from your husband." Faye wiped her nose with the back of her hand. "Speaking of, how does it feel to be a married woman?"

Faye was done talking about herself.

I couldn't blame her.

It was easy to talk about other people instead of seeing yourself and what you thought were mistakes you made.

The more she did it, though, the sooner she was going to be able to forgive herself.

God knew we didn't blame Faye for the gym explosion.

Now it was Faye's turn to figure that out.

*

Chapter Twenty-Four

Throttle

Dove was laid out on her stomach next to me, and I drew lazy circles on her bare back.

"I'm worried about her."

"Who?" I asked.

"Faye. I don't really know her, but I can see how upset she is. She blames herself for the explosion."

"She shouldn't. How was she supposed to know the dude was that unhinged that he was going to try to kill her after he broke up with her?" It wasn't Faye's fault what happened. "She needs to stop thinking about the dude. He's not worth her time."

"That was the perfect answer," Dove sighed. "You may be a little rough around the edges, Throttle, but you always say the right thing."

"Then I guess you better keep me around, doll."

She rolled away onto her side and faced me. She mimicked me by propping her hand up under her head, and a lazy, content smile played on her lips. "I plan on it. I've grown rather fond of you."

"Right back at you, doll."

She leaned into me and pressed a kiss to my lips. "I'm glad we found each other."

"Without your crazy dad talking you into spying on us, we might not have ever happened."

"See," she laughed. "That is looking at the glass half full. We need to teach Faye how to do that. And I don't really want to talk about my dad. I called him today, and he only had ten seconds of his time to give me before he babbled something about needing to get to work." She waved her hand in the air. "Back to Faye."

"I'm not really into talking about Faye or your dad while I've got you naked in my bed."

She rolled her eyes. "You've already had me twice tonight, Throttle. I was hoping we could talk."

"We are," I grunted.

She traced her finger over my lips. "What's your real name?"

"Jethro."

She blinked slowly.

"Doll?"

"I'm processing this, Throttle," she muttered. "I expected you to put up a fight or something about telling me, and you just blurted out Jethro."

I shrugged. My name wasn't cool, but that's what it was. "You asked, I answered."

"Is it always going to be that easy between us?" I asked.

Her eyes connected with mine. "I'd like to think so, though I'm sure there is going to come a time when you piss me off, and I tell you to shove it where the sun doesn't shine."

I couldn't help but laugh. "I can't wait for that day, doll."

"You're crazy," she giggled.

"Only about you, Dove."

"We do seem to make a pretty good pair, huh?"

I nodded. "Dice and Pirate were giving me shit about falling for you. They thought I was too much of a son of a bitch to land you."

She rolled her eyes. "Then I guess that makes you a lucky son of a bitch." She tipped her head to the side. "Though I like to call you my Romeo."

"That stuck with you when Max said it, huh?" I asked.

"Adalee said it, Max just repeated it. And yes, it did stick with me."

"Our ending is going to be a hell of a lot better than Romeo and Juliet's, doll."

She pressed a long, searing kiss to my lips and pushed me onto my back. "You better believe it, Throttle. We're headed straight for our own epic love story."

"The road may be bumpy for a bit, doll. We've got a cloud looming over our heads until we catch

Anthony and figure out what Boone and Gibbs have headed our way," I reminded her.

She shrugged and straddled my waist. "My life has never been a walk in the park, Throttle. As long as we're together, we'll be fine."

"I must be a lucky son of a bitch, doll."

She nodded and leaned down. "I prefer my Romeo. You're my Romeo, and I wouldn't have it any other way."

A-fucking-men.

*

Chapter Twenty-Five

Yarder

"She's in the parts storeroom."

"Are you sure?" Olive asked.

"Yeah. She walked in there half an hour ago."

"Isn't the garage closed for lunch?" Olive asked.

I was sick of being asked fucking questions all of the time. I rocked back in my chair and watched a car pull into the parking lot. "Yeah, we're closed for an hour, Olive."

"When are you going to come back to the clubhouse? Sloane and Dove wanted to watch a movie, and we wanted to see if Faye wanted to watch with us."

"You can ask her when we come back to the clubhouse." I watched a woman get out of the backseat of the car, but then the car drove off. We didn't have any customers scheduled to pick up their cars, so I didn't know who would be dropped off right now.

"When is that?" Olive asked.

"When I finish up what I'm doing." I stood and moved to the window of my office.

"What are you doing?"

"God damn, Olive. We'll be in the clubhouse in five minutes, okay?" I ended the call and tossed the phone on my desk.

I could see why Faye wanted some time to herself if Olive was on her ass all of the time like she was on mine.

The woman who had gotten out of the car turned to look at the garage.

Poppy.

What in the hell was she doing here? She had dropped off her car this morning, saying the weird orca whale sound was back, and asked if we could look at it.

I didn't know how that could be since Dice put a whole new rear end in her car, but I told her we could get to it tomorrow. I thought for sure she was going to need a ride while we had her car, but she said a friend could drive her if it was only going to take a day to fix it.

Maybe she was confused and thought we were going to look at her car today?

I walked out the front door, leaving Faye in the parts storeroom, and called to Poppy. "You need something, Poppy?"

She shielded her eyes from the sun. "You guys are closed?" she asked.

I nodded. "Every day for lunch."

"That's good."

I tipped my head to the side. "Did you need something?"

She winced and looked at the garage bays. "Where is my car?"

"Dice drove it into bay two."

Her eyes snapped to mine. "I messed up, Yarder," she called.

"What are you talking about?" I demanded.

She shook her head. "Things were piling up on me, and my rent was coming due, and I didn't have the money."

I didn't understand why she was standing in the parking lot telling me this. I knew money was more than tight for Poppy, and I had done everything I could to make it easy for her to pay back the garage. "You need money?" I asked.

"I did, but they offered to pay me if I just drove my car here. Like enough money to where I would never have to worry about money for the rest of my life."

I tipped my head to the car. "What are you talking about?"

"I did it this morning, but then I got scared, and now I'm here, but it's too late."

My mind frantically tried to keep up with what Poppy was saying. "Who paid you to bring your car here?" I asked.

She motioned for me to come closer. "This guy. I had never seen him before, but he said all I had to do was get my car in the garage and the money would be in my account within the hour. The money is there, but I can't do this. I don't want to do this," she screamed.

I looked back at the garage. What the fuck was she talking about?

"They did something to my car, Yarder," she cried. "I needed the money, and I didn't know what to do. But I don't want whatever they did to happen anymore. I needed the money," she cried. Tears streaked down her cheeks, and she ran towards the garage. "Just give me my car back, and–."

Her words died in her throat when the garage exploded, and the force of the explosion threw us backward.

Time seemed to slow, I slammed into an empty car waiting to be worked on, while Poppy flew into a motorcycle also waiting to be worked on.

Debris flew into the air, and flames bellowed out where the roof of the garage had been. The four bays of the garage were gone. Leveled to the ground. The wall of my office closest to the first garage bay was gone, and my chair had been blasted a few feet away from me.

My vision blurred, and I clumsily swiped my eyes.

"Yarder!" someone yelled.

The world tilted, and I struggled to get on my feet. I fell forward and slammed down on all fours. Blood pooled in my mouth, and I spat it onto the ground. "Poppy," I whispered. Blood dripped down my face and blurred my vision. I fell to the side and looked at the garage.

I struggled to see and saw three figures running toward me.

The shitstorm had arrived.

Get ready for *My Hero* coming March 29th, 2024!

Coming Soon

Beauty and the Grump
December 12th, 2023

A Moo Christmas
Fallen Lords MC Series
Book 11
December 25th

Blake Marshall Says He Needs Me
He Says Series
Book 3
January 19th, 2023

His Claim
Banachi Family Series
Book 2
January 29th, 2023

About the Author

Wall Street Journal and USA Today bestselling author Winter Travers is a devoted wife, mother, and aunt-turned-author born and raised in Wisconsin. After a brief stint in South Carolina, following her heart to chase the man who is now her hubby, they retreated up North to the changing seasons and to the place they now call home.

Winter spends her days writing happily ever afters and her nights being a karate mom hauling her son to practices and tournaments. She also has an addiction to anything MC-related, puppies and baking.

Winter loves to stay connected with her readers. Don't hesitate to reach out and contact her.

Facebook
Instagram
Website
Mailing List
BookBub

Check out the first chapter of
Wilder Presley Says He Loves Me

Chapter One

He's back...

Shelby Lyn

"He's back."

I snagged the last roll of black ribbon and dropped it into my basket.

"I saw him this morning at the diner. When he walked right by, I was getting my two scrambled eggs with wheat toast and maple sausage." Missy clicked her tongue. "He looked as fine as fireworks on the fourth of July out on Mason Lake, let me tell you."

My eyes searched the shelf for the second time hoping for more black ribbon to magically appear. "Maybe they have more black ribbon in the back," I mumbled. I needed at least five more yards to ensure I had enough to finish the wreath Mrs. Baxter ordered. Halloween was fast approaching, and I needed to get a jump on my yearly orders.

"Shelby Lyn." Missy snapped her fingers in my face. "Have you heard a word I've said?"

I stepped back and swatted her hand out of my face. "Yeah, you ate your breakfast this morning, and it was as good as the fourth of July fireworks."

Missy scoffed. "You missed the important part."

Missy spoke a mile a minute, and while I'm sure most of what she said was necessary to someone somewhere, most of the time, I tuned her out. After almost twenty years of friendship, I learned that if I missed something important that came out of her mouth, she tended to return to it until I heard her. This was one of those times. "Then tell me the important part while we wait for Jack to get his ass out of the backroom and help me."

"You know he's probably reading the old *Playboys* back there." Missy visibly shivered. "Thank god I never had a boy. I don't think I could have handled the crusty socks and forty-minute showers."

"Missy. Did you need to go there?" Dear god in heaven. I did not need that mental picture painted in my brain. "I doubt Jack is doing anything in the backroom. Please, he's eighteen. I hope he can control himself till he gets off work."

Missy shrugged. "Girl, you remember how boys were when we were eighteen. Horn dogs looking to rut."

"Uh, rut?" Was she talking about men or deer? *Sometimes the lines did blur.*

She scoffed and grabbed the dark blue ribbon. "Dad was watching the hunting channel last time I stopped by. What about this one?"

I shook my head. "It's navy."

"Nonsense. This is black," she insisted.

I grabbed the ribbon from her and set it back on the shelf. "It's navy, and it won't work." The backroom door swung open, and Jack walked out. "There's Jack."

"Oh lordy. See, he's tucking his shirt in." Missy hissed. "Whatever you do, do not touch his hands," she advised.

"Jack," I called. "Can you check to see if there is any more one-inch black ribbon in the back?"

Jack gave me a two-fingered salute and backtracked to the backroom.

"Gonna be ten minutes before he surfaces again. You gave him an excuse to read a few more pages," Missy laughed.

"You're a nut, Missy." I moved over to the selection of orange ribbons and tried to figure out which shade would be perfect. It needed to be bright, but not neon bright.

"Can we get back to what we were talking about before?"

"Your breakfast? It must have been pretty good if you want to keep talking about it." I fingered a light shade of orange and wondered if it would clash with the dark shadow of orange I already had at home. Mrs. Baxter was as sweet as pie, but she would have a bird if the colors weren't right for her fall wreath.

Missy scoffed. "Wilder Presley is back, Shelby," she shouted.

I dropped the light orange ribbon, and Missy's words hit me like bullets to my head. "Uh, what?" There was no way she had just said *that*.

No.

No, no, no.

Missy snapped her fingers in my face. "Now you're gonna listen, huh?" she laughed. She shook her head and turned to the rack of ribbon. "What if you did a dark purple instead of black?" she suggested.

I grabbed her shoulder and spun her back to face me. "We're not going to talk about ribbon right now," I spat.

"You're about a minute behind on your shock, Shelby. I'm over having to tell you about Wilder."

"I was listening all along," I muttered.

"Wilder Presley is back in Adams, Shelby Lyn, and you look like you saw a ghost."

I glared at Missy. "I heard you the first time you said it."

Missy cackled. "Second time I said it, you heard, but I had to repeat it because the look you get when I say his name says so much."

I didn't get a look when she said his name. There was no reason why I would get a look. *None.* "Where is Jack with my ribbon?" I grumbled.

"So you're just going to act like I didn't tell you *the* Wilder Presley is home?" Missy smirked. "You can't act like this with me, Shelby. You told me what you said the day he left." She wagged her finger in my face. "I have known you for nineteen years and one hundred ten days."

I rolled my eyes. I wasn't acting anyway, just like I hadn't had a look when she said Wilder's name. "And this isn't his home," I insisted. "When you leave for more than nine years, the place you go to becomes your home."

"Is that a rule?" Missy questioned.

"Here ya go," Jack called. He held up three rolls of black ribbon. "These are the last of them." He made his way to me, and I grabbed the rolls from him.

"Thanks." I nodded to the orange ribbon. "I need to grab a couple of rolls of orange. I'll meet you at the register."

Jack nodded. "Sounds good."

I grabbed two shades of orange and hoped they would work for the wreath, but my mind was too wound up about Wilder to even notice what I grabbed.

"Shelby," Missy called.

My eyes darted to her. "What?"

"What is going on in that head of yours right now?" she demanded.

I shrugged and dropped the orange ribbon into my basket. "I think I have two days to finish this wreath, and then I need to start thinking about the Christmas wreaths for the church while I work on the twenty other orders I have for fall or Halloween wreaths. I'm busy, Missy."

Missy tipped her head to the side and crossed her arms over her chest. "You are so full of shit, girlfriend. The man you had a crush on all of your life is back in town, and you're going to tell me you're thinking about wreaths? That you didn't tell him you loved him?"

I nodded my head. "Yes, you will believe that because you are my best friend, and you know I don't want to have this conversation at the craft store. And I told him I loved him as a friend. It was a "Have a great life, buddy. I love you." Turning on my heel, I headed to where Jack stood behind the check-out counter.

"You know I'm just going to come over to your house after I get off of work," Missy called after me.

I raised my hand over my head. "I wouldn't expect anything less from you, Missy." Missy had been my best friend for almost twenty years. She had moved to Adams when we were both ten and had become one of my close friends that summer.

"You want wine or hard booze?" she asked.

I needed a damn tranquilizer if what she had told me was true. "Bring the Southern," I replied.

"Woo, wee," Missy chuckled. "This is going to be a fun night."

I rolled my eyes and set my basket on the check-out counter. "You wouldn't by chance have a bottle of booze behind the counter, would you, Jack?" I blew my hair out of my face and sighed.

"Uh, well, I think my dad might have a bottle hidden in his office," Jack stammered. "I could see if I could get you a glass."

Oh, sweet Jack. He was just a little too naïve for his good.

I nodded to the basket. "I think I can make it home without a glass. Thank you, though."

Jack looked visibly relieved.

Five minutes later, I was sitting behind the steering wheel of my truck and closed my eyes.

Wilder Presley was back in town.

Twelve years ago, I had watched that man drive out of my life with not so much as a backward glance. He had broken my heart that day, and he hadn't even known it.

Wilder Presley was back, and so were all those feelings I thought I had buried.

No amount of Southern was going to make this any easier.

*

Check out the first chapter of
Drop a Gear & Disappear

Chapter One

Quinn

A lady in the streets and a freak in the bed…

"Come with me, baby."

Kimber rolled into my side. "I'll pass."

I looked down at her naked body and ran my fingers over her smooth, flawless skin. "You're gonna have to come there one day."

"But today is not that day, Quinn."

"It's Gear, baby."

She snorted and tipped her head back to look at me. "Okay, Quinn."

I fucking hated my name, yet Kimber insisted on calling me it even though I finally got my road name from the Rolling Devils. "You gotta learn to tolerate the club, baby. I know you don't like it, but you gotta not hate it."

"Mmhmm," she hummed under her breath and laid her head back on my shoulder. Her hand slid across the expanse of my chest, and her fingers trailed over the tattoo of an eagle holding a skull. "But you don't need to leave just yet," she whispered.

"Soon."

"Maybe I need to remind you what will be waiting for you while you're fetching beers for all of your club buddies."

"I do more than that."

"Right," she drawled.

At least on normal days, I did more than that. On nights like tonight, I did basically just fetch beer and booze the whole time. "So what exactly are you going to do to make me not forget about you?"

She rolled onto her back and slowly raised her hands over her head. "It's more like what are you going to do."

I turned onto my side and slid my hand down between her tits. "Daddy's choice?" I whispered.

Her eyes flared with desire.

I was a lucky fucker to have Kimber in my bed.

The saying "a lady in the streets and a freak in the bed" was Kimber to a T.

During the day, she worked at a doctor's office where she answered phones and dealt with bitchy ass people with a smile on her lips, and at night, she was my naughty little minx who couldn't get enough of me.

I grabbed her by the waist and flipped her over onto her stomach. "On your knees, ass in the air."

She scampered up to her knees and wiggled her ass at me. I moved behind her, my knees between her legs, and slapped her ass. "Always hungry for my cock," I growled.

She looked over her shoulder at me with her bottom lip between her teeth and nodded her head. "Always," she whispered.

My hand wrapped around my cock, and I stroked up and down with my eyes never leaving hers. "Greedy pussy."

She reared back and bumped her ass against my hand. "Stop talking and start doing."

I gripped the globe of her ass and parted her cheeks. Her pussy was dripping, and the bud of her ass begged to be fucked. "Anything I want, baby?"

"I guess that all depends on what time you need to leave," she replied coyly.

I knew I didn't have the time to fuck her properly. She was trying to distract me from going to the club, but I couldn't miss the party. I pressed my dick against the entrance to her pussy and slowly pushed in. "Your ass is mine later tonight," I promised.

She reared back again, her ass grinding against me. "Promises, promises," she muttered.

Damn right, it was a fucking promise. It was one I planned on keeping, too. I grabbed a handful of her hair and pulled her head back. "I'm gonna fuck you so hard, you aren't going to be able to get out of bed the whole time I'm gone."

"Yes," she hissed.

I put a hand on her hip and thrust deep. "Who do you belong to, Kimber?" I demanded.

"You," she breathed out.

"Say my name."

A sultry laugh fell from her lips. "Does one name get me a fucking and the other a spanking?"

"Damn straight, baby. Choose carefully."

She rubbed her ass against me and flexed the walls of her pussy around my dick. "As fun as a spanking sounds, I need your dick."

I slowly pulled out then slammed back into her. "Like that? You want it hard?"

She groaned and shook her head. "Yes, Daddy."

I let go of her hair and grabbed her hips.

She dropped her head to the mattress and braced her arms. "Please, Gear. Fuck me."

She spoke the words she knew would drive me crazy and give her exactly what she wanted.

With each thrust of my hips, she moaned my name.

My fingers dug into her hips as I held her still and drove into her. "Tell me again," I grunted.

"I'm yours," she gasped. "I'm yours, Gear."

I felt her climax climbing and moved faster. "Play with yourself, baby." I was going to come soon, and I wanted her pussy to milk every last drop of cum from me.

Her hand snaked between her legs. "Gear, please," she pleaded. "Fuck me."

While her fingers stroked her clit, my dick pounded her pussy.

"I'm...I'm coming," she whimpered. "Gear...please."

Her pussy contracted around my dick as her orgasm washed over her, and she ripped my release from me. "Fuck yeah," I grunted. "Take it all, baby."

She panted my name then buried her face in the pillow.

The final tremors rocked through me, and I fell onto the mattress next to her.

She dropped the rest of the way and partially rolled into me.

I threw an arm over her and pulled her close. "Sure you don't want to come with me?" I asked again. "We could find a room at the clubhouse and find the time to do that all over again."

She laughed and shook her head. "Or I could just stay here, eat some pizza, and sleep until you get home."

"It's gonna be late." I didn't expect to leave the clubhouse 'til well into the morning.

"Just wake me up when you get home."

She wasn't going to budge on this. I had been a prospect for the club four months, and she refused to even step foot at the clubhouse. "One day, I'm going to get you to come to a party."

She scoffed. "But that day is not today," she laughed.

I pressed a kiss to the side of her head and rolled out of bed. She pulled the blanket over her body and turned onto her back. "You didn't need to cover up."

She rolled her eyes and fluffed the pillow under her head. "Last I checked, if you're not in this bed, then you don't have a say about what I'm wearing or doing."

I grabbed the blanket and tugged it down her body 'til I could see her tits. "Is that so?"

She grabbed the blanket to tug it up, but I didn't let it go. "You're gonna be late, Quinn," she tried to reason.

"I'm already late, Kimber. My ass should have been on my bike half an hour ago, but your greedy pussy kept me in bed."

She scooted down the bed and managed to get under the covers enough to conceal her body from me. "Well, this pussy is staying in bed cause I had a long day at work and since you just fucked me twice, I think a nap is needed before I order pizza."

"A nap and pizza, huh?" That did seem like a good night, but the club couldn't be put off. I let go of the blanket and bent to pick up my clothes. "Save me a slice, and don't put fucking olives on it."

She snuggled under the blanket and watched me get dressed. "How many people are going to be there tonight?"

This was the fourth large party the club had since I had started prospecting, and each one kept getting bigger than the last. "I think a shit-ton. I don't get to sit in on the meetings, but Mud had mentioned another club was coming in for the night."

"Still can't believe the guy who is your sponsor goes by the name Mud."

I shrugged on my shirt. "Baby, I told you road names can be anything. You should be happy and realize I was lucky to get a name like Gear and not Mud or Bug." I pulled on my socks and then my pants.

She wrinkled her nose. "Doesn't mean I have to like it."

I sat down on the edge of the mattress and pulled on my shoes. "But you don't have to bust my balls about it all of the time," I reminded her.

"I know," she sighed. "I promise I'll come to the next party with you. I just don't want to go to one of these and then be left all alone because you have some obligation to grab someone a beer every five minutes."

I stood up and turned to look down at her. "You're really going to go to the next one?" I asked, surprised. I really didn't think I was ever going to be able to get her to come to the clubhouse.

She nodded. "Only for you, though. I'm not interested in making friends with the other chicks."

"They're called ol' ladies, Kimber," I chuckled. "And I happen to know when the next party is."

"Oh God," she laughed. "I have time to look forward to dreading going."

I shook my head. "You won't have to wait long. Tomorrow night is another party."

Her jaw dropped. "Wait…what?" she squawked. "I can't…you didn't…"

She knew there wasn't a way in hell that I was going to let her go back on her promise of coming to the next party. I leaned down and pressed a kiss to her lips. "Get some rest, baby. You're going to need it for the party tomorrow."

I strutted out of the room and straight out of our apartment.

Kimber may not like the club, but she was going to start coming to these damn parties with me.

She had said she would, and I wasn't going to let her go back on her word.

*

Printed in Great Britain
by Amazon